OPERATOR 5:
THE DAWN THAT SHOOK THE WORLD

# SECRET SERVICE OPERATOR #5™

## AMERICA'S UNDERCOVER ACE

# THE DAWN THAT SHOOK THE WORLD

*By Curtis Steele*

POPULAR PUBLICATIONS • 2024

PUBLISHING HISTORY

"The Dawn That Shook the World" originally appeared in the November/December, 1938 (Vol. 11, No. 2) issue of *Operator #5* magazine. Copyright © 2024 by Argosy Communications, Inc. All rights reserved.

# CHAPTER 1
# THE INFERNAL MACHINE

T HICK, HEAVY smoke funneled up from the tall chimneys, rising straight in the still air until it flattened out in a dark, grayish-black cloud that seemed to shroud the sky from horizon to horizon. Beneath that cloud hummed a beehive of industry.

Pittsburgh was itself again—the big steel mills running at full blast, day and night, turning out the finely tempered metal so necessary now for rebuilding and rearming America. In less than three years, since the collapse of the Purple Empire and expulsion of the last of the rapacious invaders from American soil, this bustling city had sprung up from shattered, gutted ruins.

In this incredibly short period a defeated, enslaved people had thrown off their shackles and sprung to the task of reconstruction.

This magnificent feat of rehabilitation owed its accomplishment chiefly to the dogged determination and tireless energy of a man whose zeal for rebuilding was second only to his patriotic vigilance. Twice during those danger-fraught years, when the reborn nation was so unprepared to match strength with the powerful nations of Europe and Asia, his constant watchfulness had enabled him to nip certain foreign invasion in the very bud.

Operator 5 his fellow citizens called this man whose eagle eyes seemed to encompass every corner of America—and even

beyond, to distant shores wherever danger was brewing. In Washington, close to Triumvir Andrew Warren, Operator 5 had his headquarters; but his countrymen somehow felt he was all over, his alert eyes missing no sign of trouble, no matter how skillfully it might be concealed....

And that had been true!

But now....

## THE DAWN THAT SHOOK THE WORLD

Thick smoke funneled up from the chimneys of the steel mills, and out of the employees' entrances, serpented other dark streams—grimy, tired-looking workers with lunch boxes on their arms, shoulders stooped, faces dull and apathetic. Hard-working men who had little time for play—for anything but work and the problems of existence. For this reawakening America was once more a pioneer country where life was hard and exacting.

Almost listlessly they filed out toward the streets—until suddenly an electric spark seemed to galvanize them. Stooped shoulders squared, dull eyes gleamed, relaxed faces became taut and vulpine. For an instant their eyes flashed mute understanding to the dungaree-clad man who lounged just inside the mill gate, and then they passed on.

"Eight-thirty—without fail!" the man mumbled over and over again, and each time the result was the same—as if he had shot an elixir into those tired, shambling figures. "Eight-thirty—"

Midway along that outpouring stream came a small, wiry figure—younger and half a head shorter than most of his mates. Grime and sweat had coated his face so that the freckles which covered it were almost buried. But the stains of the day's toil were not able to hide the rakish tilt of his short pug-nose or the gray-blue eyes that were keenly alert despite their pretended listlessness.

"Eight-thirty—without fail!" droned into this youth's ear, and his head nodded ever so slightly in acknowledgment. But the moment he was out onto the street his eyes kindled with excitement.

For a moment he looked around him. He exchanged a knowing glance with another worker who stood smoking a cigarette nearby, then started off across town. His destination was an unpretentious rooming-house, where he climbed to the third floor and repeated two short, sharp knocks on a door at the front of the building.

IT WAS opened cautiously by a young woman, whose severely combed hair and simple business dress valiantly strove to conceal the fresh beauty of her finely featured face.

"Thank God, you're home, Di," the visitor greeted as he pushed past her and dropped into a chair in the cheaply furnished living-room. "They're meeting tonight—and this is a 'without fail' call. Things are just about ready to pop—I know it!"

"Tonight, Tim?" Diane Elliot's tone was worried, her brow wrinkled in a frown. "So soon?—I *was* hoping they would wait, that we would have more time. Jimmy should be here...."

Her clouded eyes met his flashing glance, held it. For a long moment they were speechless, these two who knew each other so well. But the perfect communion of their eyes was more revealing than mere words. In both minds was a single thought, a single face and figure—Jimmy Christopher's.

To Diane that face was the face of a sweetheart, the man she intended to marry as soon as a troubled, seething world would grant America the boon of lasting peace. More than that, he was a comrade, a leader with whom she had shared countless dangers, to whom she had been beholden for her life time and again.

To Tim Donovan it was the face of a friend, of a captain—one

who seemed little less than a god.
Ever since that night, years ago,
when Tim, a ragged, hungry news-
boy shivering in a dark hallway, had
saved Jimmy Christopher from a
criminal's bullet, Jimmy had been
his ideal, the very motivation of his
existence—a being upon whom he
lavished his trust, admiration and
devotion.

To both Diane and Tim, members of that close little band
who had fought at Operator 5's side all through the Purple
Wars and the troubled years that followed, Jimmy Christopher
was the answer to America's every need—her most dependable
safeguard in time of trouble.

"I wish to heaven he were here, Di," Tim said fervently. "If
you get word to him immediately, he may be able to make it in
time. Hal Rawson is keeping watch at the plant. He will let you
know if anything else comes up. I'll be back here as soon as the
meeting is over."

Diane stared at him silently, tensely—seemingly on the verge
of trying to stop him. "It isn't fair!" she burst forth suddenly, as
her eyes snapped with anger. "The moment we get a breathing
spell, the moment the way to peace and happiness seems clear,
trouble has to crop up again. Will there never be any end to it?"

Tensely she strode to the window and stood looking out at the
smoke-blanketed sky. When she turned back, her face was bleak.

"Here we are working day and night to perfect our armaments for protection against the wolves that surround us on every side—and meanwhile the jackals at home are gathering to hamstring us and pull us down from behind. Jimmy can handle the foreign nations, but these traitorous trouble-makers at home—they are stabbing him in the back, Tim!"

Tim Donovan's knuckles whitened as he clutched the doorknob, and his usually good-natured face set in a harsh mask. Well he realized the truth of what she said—realized it even more that he had admitted. Three weeks ago, when he and Diane had come to Pittsburgh and found work in the steel mill and one of the mill offices, he had thought that the unrest Operator 5 sensed in this section was nothing more than the work of some irresponsible agitator. But gradually he had begun to realize that there was more to it than that. He discovered unmistakable signs of a far-reaching organization that was stirring up dissension among the workers and feeding on their discontent.

A week ago his fears had been fully substantiated when the fellow workers, whom he had been cultivating, introduced him into the brotherhood of the New Dawn—an outfit that planned to take over not only the government of the United States but the rule of the entire world!

"More than one traitorous renegade has tried to stab Operator 5 in the back," Tim gritted. "Jimmy knows how to take care of snakes of that sort. But it's our job to run them out of their holes so that he can identify them. That's what I want to do tonight."

Tim's words were no braggadocio. More than once he had proved that he did not know the meaning of fear, and now he was confidently setting out for a rendezvous where his identification as one of Operator 5's men would mean his death.

As Diane watched him go, a persistent uneasiness tugged at her heart. Almost, as her eyes followed his lithe young figure down the street, she could see disaster dogging his footsteps....

With an effort she took a grip on herself. Carefully, she coded a message to Operator 5, then took it to the telegraph office, to dispatch it to the dummy New York address from which it would be quickly forwarded to Washington.

"You're just in time to take this message that arrived for you ten minutes ago, Miss Seymour," the operator smiled as he identified her—and as Diane took the yellow envelope from his hand the premonition of disaster clutched at her heart.

NOT UNTIL she was back in her room did she dare attempt to decode the telegram—and as the message began to take shape before her, her vague fears became starkly definite. The message was from Jerry Tarbell, one of Jimmy Christopher's men who had been investigating the reported unrest in Cleveland.

"Richmond and Daley killed this afternoon; Hawkins disappeared," it read. "Have discovered that a vital leak has revealed identity of our complete roster, in other cities as well as here. I was trailed to this office and may not be able to get out of it all alive. Good luck to you!"

Richmond and Daley murdered, Hawkins mysteriously disappeared—that just about wiped out Operator 5's Cleveland staff. And the identity of the rest of his men was uncovered.... That meant that Tim Donovan was walking blindly into a death-trap!

For a moment Diane sat stunned at her writing table as the full significance of that message percolated into her consciousness. Then quick plans began to formulate in her brain and she rose from the table, giving herself a hurried inspection in a mirror.

Tim had to be warned somehow. Perhaps she could head him off before he reached the meeting place. Perhaps she could contact Hal Rawson and have him carry the warning. Some way—there *must* be a way to stop him before it would be too late!

Subconsciously, she stopped at the window, peered out into the street—and in that fraction of a second her swift glance encountered a pair of eyes staring up at her window. No accidental stare, she knew that instantly. The fellow was half-slouched in a doorway across the way, watching the house—*watching her window.*

She, too, had been uncovered, and her death watch had been set! If she attempted to leave, she would be seized or killed. Yet she *had* to get out of that building! She must reach Tim no matter at what cost!

Out of a maelstrom of desperate plans came one that *must* work. Handbag on her arm, she went out into the hall and down the two flights of stairs to the street. Hesitantly, she stepped out of the front door, glanced warily up and down the street—to become suddenly transfixed with terror when she caught a glimpse of the watcher opposite. Her eyes widened, and a scream seemed to hover on her lips. Then she appeared to recover control of herself and dived back through the doorway.

For a long moment she crouched behind the wooden-paneled

door—then her up-raised arm tensed above her head. Footsteps were clicking across the street, a hand grasped the doorknob, a dark figure lunged in, sprang to the foot of the stairs… then went down with half-uttered groan as her blackjack crashed against his skull.

Quickly Diane was standing over him, grasping his shoulders, dragging him upstairs. Fortunately, he was not a heavy man, weighing little more than she. Yet her muscles were aching, her body bathed in perspiration, by the time she had dragged him into her room and sunk, panting, on a chair.

SOME DISTANCE beyond the steel mills and adjoining freight yards was a large brick building which the company executives had presented to the workers' welfare organization to be used as an auditorium. For lack of time and inclination, the workmen had been neglecting it lately, but now it had found a new purpose. It was meeting place of the votaries of the New Dawn.

From a vantage point some distance from the entrance, Tim Donovan watched while more than five hundred workmen approached the building and slipped furtively, or strode defiantly, through the doorway. More than five hundred… and still they came.

When he recognized one of his shop-mates who had vouched for his admission to the organization, Tim sauntered out and joined him. Together they passed the alert-eyed sentries in the wide foyer and stepped into the already crowded hall. That hall buzzed with the drone of excited voices and was studded with eager-eyed, grim-lipped faces.

Gone was the lethargy that had marked many of these men a few hours before. Now they were keyed up, expectantly waiting for their leaders to take their places on the flag-decorated platform, individually voicing their discontent.

"Forgotten men... slaves of capital... underprivileged ones... the men Andy Warren hasn't time for... the underdog's day on top... the end of poverty and slavery...." One after the other Tim caught those familiar phrases babbling from their lips. When he looked searchingly into their faces, he saw that these men were like parrots, mouthing the catch-phrases that had been poured into their ears. But they were no less dangerous for being stupid. In the hands of wily, unscrupulous leaders, these men could be worked up to a murderous frenzy, could be goaded on and incited to almost any excess.

Who were those leaders? That was what Tim wanted to know. But when the chairman and his aids had taken their places on the rostrum, he was still in the dark. These men were agitators, professional organizers—*not* the brains behind the New Dawn. They were the men who had been fomenting the discontent in the mills—*not* the ones who had dictated this program of moral sabotage.

Now the chairman was rapping for order. A bulldog-faced man, he stood behind a large speaker's table that was draped with the banner of the New Dawn—a black flag with a blazing sun rising between Stygian hills and girding the sky with orange streamers. While he strove to make himself heard, yellow-uniformed attendants were filing through the packed crowd, passing out paper cups and filling them with a crimson liquid.

Tim was at her side, fighting off that mob!

Tim held his cup in his hand and eyed his neighbors surreptitiously. He had heard of this drink, but this was first experience with it. He was tempted to pour the contents of his cup on the floor—except that it would be certain to attract attention.

"A toast!" the chairman's voice boomed out in the suddenly quiet hall. "To the New Dawn—that comes *tomorrow!*"

Silently, those cups were drained, and then the walls of that hall fairly trembled with the triumphant howl rising from nearly a thousand throats. "The New Dawn!"

To Tim's ears, their voracious cry had the sound of a wolf-pack closing in on the kill. These human wolves were closing in on their own defenseless country—were howling for the blood of America!

Red rage coursed through Tim's veins. He could feel it pounding in his wrists, throbbing in his temples. He wanted to tear into these traitors, wanted to batter them into submission, slaughter them... and suddenly he realized that this raging inferno in his brain was not natural. His blood *was* on fire, his reason wildly inflamed—by that toast he had drunk and the drug it must have contained.

When he glanced at his neighbors, he was certain of it. They were blazing-eyed, snarling-lipped. Worked up to near-hysteria, they were hanging on every word that came from the platform, cursing their approval.

"Our day is at hand!" the chairman shouted. "Here is what we have been waiting for!"

As he spoke, his assistants seized the ends of a huge tarpaulin that had been spread over a shapeless mound behind the speaker's stand, yanked it clear—and revealed case after case of rifles. U.S. Army rifles of the latest pattern, still in the cases in which they had come from the factory! U.S. Government weapons which would be used to overthrow the government itself!

Somehow these devils must have raided an arms shipment—or looted a government arsenal! Appalled, Tim stared at that mound of weapons and at the cases of ammunition behind the guns.

Then again the chairman's rasping voice filled his ears.

"This is only a small part," he was shouting. "We have plenty more—machine-guns, artillery, everything that we need. The New Dawn is at hand. But before our victorious sun rises, there are certain precautions we must take—here tonight! While we have been planning and working for the day of the working man's emancipation there have been those among us who have been striving to undermine our efforts. There have been traitors among us—and there are traitors here now!" he howled rabidly. "Operator 5's men have been among you daily. They are here in this hall tonight!"

TIM FELT the hot blood cool in his veins. Muscles tensing, his hand edged toward his shoulder-holstered revolver. He would be overwhelmed and torn to pieces by this drug-maddened mob, but at least he would take that devil on the platform to the grave with him....

But at that moment the chairman whirled—and out from the wings of the platform-stage came four men, dragging between them the bound form of Hal Rawson!

"Here is one of them!" the chairman shouted, as he leered

13

into Rawson's tight-lipped face. "And now he is going to identify his mates!"

At his signal, a curious-looking contraption was rolled out
onto the stage by half a dozen yellow-shirted assistants. A
ponderous apparatus constructed of heavy iron, it appeared to
be a heavy chair with a huge, thick-spoked wheel attached to
one side of it. When it was in place, Rawson was thrust in the
chair, his legs and left arm strapped to it. Then his right arm was
fastened by heavy metal clasps to a spoke of the wheel. Grinning
evilly, the chairman faced him.

"Now," he taunted, "tell us the names of the rest of your crowd
here in Pittsburgh." A moment's pause, and then, "Very well, if
you don't know how to talk—"

He touched a button at the side of the chair, and the wheel
started to turn, twisting Rawson's arm backward until it seemed
the bones must snap.

"Once more," the torturer prodded, as he shut off the current.
"The names—or the current goes on again."

Tim could see the blood running down Rawson's chin where
his teeth bit through his lip, could see the perspiration beading
out on his face. But not a word came from the prisoner. Defiantly, he returned the chairman's stare—and the inhuman devil
pushed his thumb against the button.

Once more the wheel started backward horribly. Now the
popping-eyed crowd watched with bated breath. Ghastly stillness settled over the hall—to be broken by the fearful sound of
snapping bones!

Tim half-rose from his seat, his fingers clutching his revolver butt. Every instinct urged him to charge up to that platform, to shoot down the inhuman monster at the wheel... but a stern voice, that had the tone of Jimmy Christopher's seemed to whisper in his ear an inexorable reminder that the ordeal of an individual must not be considered when the fate of America was in jeopardy.

That was the chance Rawson had taken—the chance every undercover man took. Rawson knew now that there could be no help for him. He would be the last man to ask that a fellow-agent betray the common trust in order to aid him.

Tim rallied every argument, volleyed them at his wavering determination. He knew what he must do—but that barbarous machine *was ripping Rawson's arm out of its socket!*

Blood was spurting, flesh rending... a ghastly groan wrenched from between the gritting jaws of the sufferer. Then Tim leaped from his seat, just as another spectator sprang into the aisle and vaulted up onto the platform, gun in hand—a slim, lithe fellow with a cap tilted over one side of his face. That much Tim saw in a flash of action.

"Radzow, are you crazy?" the chairman howled, but in that moment the newcomer had reached his side. The revolver crashed down into his face, beat him back in a bloody pulp, as Hal Rawson's head sagged forward limply on his chest.

For an instant, that sudden onslaught held the others spellbound; then, quickened to swift action, the yellow-shirted assistants swarmed over the attacker. Twice the avenger's gun barked. Then he was beaten down onto the floor, gamely battling on his knees, clambering back to his feet.

And now the cap was knocked from his head—to release the chestnut curls of Diane Elliot, her face cleverly made up as a man's!

A thrill of pride and admiration shot through Tim Donovan and routed the panic that momentarily assailed him when he recognized her. It was Di—up there alone—facing a thousand blood-maddened beasts single-handed!

With a shout of wild exultation Tim reached her side, smashing his gun muzzle into snarling faces—punching, clawing, butting into those yellow-shirted devils who surrounded her. Some went down, some went spinning headlong off the platform, others were swept back by that savage charge. In a moment Diane was in the clear, panting at his side as she strove to catch her breath—but now every man in that crowded hall was up on his feet.

Howling their hate, they came clambering up onto the platform in a deluge of rabid faces and hurtling fists.

"Back of this infernal machine!" Tim shouted, as he dragged Diane to the shelter of the torture chair. "Fire right into them! That's our only chance!"

## CHAPTER 2
## PRELUDE TO DAWN

DUSK WAS settling over a sparsely traveled highway on the western outskirts of Pittsburgh when a rickety, weather-beaten coupé drove into a none too prosperous-looking crossroads gas station. Out of the cheap machine stepped a sandy-haired young man clad in the rough, work-stained clothes of a laborer.

"Fill 'er up." He nodded toward his gas tank, as the proprietor came up to serve him. Then, without waiting to see his order fulfilled, he stepped into the shack that housed the office and comfort station.

Once inside, the slovenly droop of his shoulders disappeared, his lackluster expression vanished. He stepped into a cubby-hole, that opened off the rear of the office, and picked up the receiver of a wall telephone. That line was a direct wire to Washington, D.C. In a few minutes, a guarded voice came over it, asking curious and apparently unrelated questions.

"Okay, Jimmy." Satisfied recognition terminated that interchange. "I certainly am glad you called. I've been wanting all day to hear from you, wondering whether you, too...."

Jimmy Christopher was quick to catch the note of anxiety, and his eyes narrowed almost imperceptibly. "What is it, Dad?" he clipped. "Bad news?"

"I'm afraid so," John Christopher admitted. "Cleveland, Cincinnati, Scranton, Wilkes-Barre—in each city our men have been spotted and killed during the past twenty-four hours. I can get no word from Columbus or Youngstown, although it is hours past the time the regular calls should have come in. Hasbrouck reports a well organized opposition in Wheeling and expects a blow-up at any minute. I think the climax is approaching, Jimmy. These killings apparently were on schedule, to clear the way...."

Jimmy Christopher's lips clenched in a thin white line as he listened to his father's report. His own suspicions were all too thoroughly confirmed. He was like a man sitting on a load of dynamite and looking vainly for the lighted fuse that would ignite it at any moment.

For several months, his agents had been picking up hints and rumors of a revolutionary organization that was breeding discontent among the factory and mill workers. Soon he had become convinced that serious trouble was brewing, and at once prepared to cope with it. Spreading his men over six states in a huge net, he had started his campaign to unmask the trouble-makers. But sitting in an office was a role that poorly fitted Operator 5. He had chafed in it until anonymous reports from an unidentified undercover man, who claimed to be in the confidence of the agitators, had located the danger center as Pittsburgh.

That was all Jimmy needed to send him into action. Incognito, he had followed his men into the affected territory, leaving his father, the retired Q-6 of American Secret Service, in charge at the Washington headquarters. Q-6 was living on borrowed time—a bullet embedded close to his heart might mean death for John Christopher at any time. Yet even though that limited his physical activity, it in no way impaired his executive ability or dulled his avid yearning to help the country he had faithfully served all his life.

"There is no ordinary agitator behind this thing, Jimmy," the old man's canny voice summed up. "From every indication, the organization is far more extensive than we realize, the directors well covered. We can only hope that they have not gotten too big a start on us—"

"They haven't, Dad," Jimmy snapped. "If they are going into action so will we." And for several minutes he outlined his plans, gave his orders. But when he put the receiver back on its hook and walked out to the battered car his blue eyes were troubled, the tired droop of his shoulders this time not entirely assumed.

Paying for his gas, he passed brief instructions to Charlie Detmer, the greasy khaki-uniformed proprietor, then headed for Pittsburgh. But before he had driven much more than a mile another idea occurred to him and he swung back toward the gas station, driving slowly as the details of the plan took form in his mind.

ABSORBED WITH his thoughts, Jimmy was almost up to the station before a subconscious alarm dinned in his brain. There was now something odd about that station—something not as it should be. And then he knew! The lamps on the gas pumps were still dark—although Detmer had been starting toward the shack to turn them on as Jimmy drove away....

Bringing his car to a noiseless stop in the shadows, a hundred feet from the station, Jimmy saw that a car was drawn up at one of the unlighted pumps. But there was nobody in it, or near it—nor was there any sign of Detmer around the place. Warily, he started forward—and then stopped stockstill a dozen steps from the shack. To his ears had come the wet sound of a choked gurgle....

That gurgle was immediately followed by the tinkle of breaking glass as one of the shack windows shattered!

Swiftly Jimmy catfooted up to another window, peering into the semi-dark interior. The heavy gloom was split by a narrow beam of light that played downward—on the blood-soaked face and horribly bashed head of Charley Detmer, sprawled on the floor!

For a moment the narrow flashlight beam shifted and was reflected from the wall sufficiently so that it dimly illumined the face of the killer—the face of Jake Horeski, one of the workmen in the shop where Jimmy held a dummy job....

Satisfied that his victim was dead, Horeski backed out of the door and closed it behind him. For an instant he paused on the threshold, and death hovered over him... but Jimmy clamped an iron grip on his burning rage. Slowly his itching finger relaxed on the trigger of his revolver, and he shoved the weapon back into its holster.

Charlie Detmer would be fully avenged, but now was not the time to settle the score for him. That bloody-handed murderer was far more valuable alive than dead.

Horeski covered the distance from the shack to his car in half a dozen swift strides, but when he drove off in the direction of the city, an inconspicuous-looking coupé trailed him. Carefully, Jimmy Christopher followed, wary lest he come close enough to be suspected and yet not lagging so far behind that Horeski could escape.

Past the steel mills Horeski drove, down through the business section of town and then to the bank of the Monongahela River, where he parked near a large river-boat moored at the quay. The electric sign over its gangplank identified the boat as a floating night-club, but at this early evening hour it seemed to be deserted.

Horeski walked up the gang-plank, strode across the deck, unchallenged, and headed for the river side of the boat. On his heels came Jimmy Christopher—so close that when he rounded the corner of the superstructure, he came face to face with Horeski.

Evil triumph gleamed in the killer's eyes as he drove his fist viciously at Jimmy's head. But before that murderous blow could land its target has vanished—and Horeski staggered back with blood streaming from his battered lips. Three blows in amazingly quick succession swept him backward. Jimmy wasted no time boxing. He dived at the fellow's middle, toppled him off his feet and tied him up in a merciless grip that held him helpless—a hold the great Zbysko had once taught the young stripling who eluded his best efforts so surprisingly.

Horeski bent almost double. A groaning curse tore from his lips… and then he sealed his own death warrant.

Out from a hip pocket holster, he plucked a heavy revolver, tried to draw a bead on Jimmy's head—and had the weapon ripped out of his grasp. For an instant it poised above his head, then crashed down into his terror-blanched face. Relentlessly, Operator 5 battered him—until he slumped to the deck in a bloody heap. Charlie Detmer's murder was avenged.

Above the bloody figure Jimmy crouched, listening to see

whether that brief struggle had been heard. Then he was padding his way softly along the deck until he reached a companionway that led forward. Now he caught the rumble of distant voices somewhere up there ahead.

LIKE A jungle cat he crept along until he was outside the salon from which the conversation came, crouching low with his ear against the closed door. It took but a few moments to tell him that he was eavesdropping on a conference of the leaders of the trouble.

He caught a satisfied chuckle from one of them. "That means everything is ready in twenty key cities. All they need is an example and they will be ready to go—and *that* example we'll give them here tomorrow in Pittsburgh. While Andy Warren is making himself President, his government will be toppling around his ears. Pittsburgh tomorrow—and the next day the revolution will sweep the country!"

"And after that Great Britain, France—the world," another voice added his evil benediction. "After that, an empire such as no man has ever ruled!"

That voice was familiar, startlingly familiar, and yet Jimmy could not place it. But he *had* to. Daringly he wedged the door open that least little bit. Now he could see that there were four or five conspirators. Three were within the range of his vision. Then he caught a glimpse of the fourth—a leonine face with a gray mustache and goatee, crowned by a mop of silvery gray hair.

This face, too, was familiar—its identity clamored at Jimmy's brain even as it eluded him. But now the import of the conference drove all other thoughts from his mind.

"The arms and ammunition are on hand?" one man asked.

"Delivered as promised," came in that familiar voice—from the man whom Jimmy could not see. "They will be distributed tonight at the welfare association hall."

"And tomorrow the forgotten men will arise and come into their own," was the answer. "Tomorrow the underdogs will take matters into their own hands and set up a new and perfect government." His voice dripped with sarcasm, contempt for the blind fools who were being tricked into betraying their country.

Jimmy's hands balled into hard fists that ached to smash into that complacent face—when some sixth sense saved his own life! He threw himself flat, just as a dark figure hurtled over him and crashed against the door.

Instantly Jimmy was on his feet—was splitting the fellow's skull with his revolver barrel. Then he dived through the doorway into the salon beyond. But that moment of uproar was sufficient for the conspirators. They were on their feet, dashing for doors, windows—any way of escape.

One of them Jimmy shot down before he was fully clear of the table. Another he drilled through the back of the head, as he was attempting to fling himself through a doorway. A third he brought down in the corridor beyond the saloon. Then he triggered a shot at the familiar gray-goateed face. But that shot missed its mark. A derisive laugh jeered back at him, echoed by a violent splash.

By the time Jimmy reached the deck and peered over the boat's side he heard only the sound of distant splashing—then even that stopped. Vainly he tried to pierce the night, but there were no lights on the river side of the vessel—and no lights on the seaplane that suddenly roared into life and sped down the river before it took to the air.

At least two of the scheming devils had gotten away, and Jimmy silently damned himself as he went back to the corpse-strewn salon. For now he had identified that leonine-faced individual as Evan Carliotti, an international mountebank and trouble-maker.

During the days of the Purple Empire, Carliotti had amassed a fortune by dealing in munitions, but the moment the empire had started to disintegrate he deserted the sinking ship. Since then he had been embroiled in half a dozen foreign insurrections and political *coups*, had been accused of all sorts of illicit dealings, with more than one price placed on his head. Yet he had managed to keep out of harm's way, no matter what happened to his luckless followers.

And now Evan Carliotti was turning his attention to America....

GRIMLY JIMMY walked from one to the other of the plotters he had downed. But his aim had been too perfect. There wasn't a spark of life in any of them. Indeed, that silent boat seemed to have been deserted by all but the dead—until he bent over the huddled figure of Jake Horeski. The murderer was sufficiently alive to glare malignantly from half-open eyes and spew a stream of vitriolic curses from blood-flecked lips.

"Operator 5—the great Operator 5!" he sneered. "America's super-spy! We picked you up the minute you reached Pittsburgh—followed you every minute—let you play your smart

24

role. You think you've won, don't you? But you're a fool... a poor little fool who will be swept away when the New Dawn breaks over Europe. You and your America will be overwhelmed, wiped out—*buried* by the avalanche! You'll be—" The crimson rush of his own blood choked that torrent of hate.

But when Jimmy turned away from the still figure he fully realized that this was no local rebellion. Not merely a plot to overthrow the government of the United States, but a gigantic, world-wide conspiracy to wipe out the world's democracies and substitute for them an unscrupulous tyranny.

It was a staggering scheme for world empire that might sweep the unsuspecting democracies off their feet even before the alarm could be given. Tomorrow, the day on which Andrew Warren was to relinquish the title of Triumvir to be inaugurated as the fortieth President of the United States, would see the launching of the revolt in America!

But, thank God, there might still be time to spike that treacherous outbreak—and this boat was the place to start....

THE LEADEN death that blasted from Tim Donovan's revolver caught the leaders of the infuriated New Dawn mob as they came spilling over the edge of the auditorium platform— caught and hurled them back on top of their fellows. Instantly Diane grasped his idea and crouched beside him, her back to his, pouring a lethal hail around the other side of the diabolical chair in which Hal Rawson's body sprawled inertly.

Screams of pain and wild yells of terror suddenly mingled with the blood-lusting clamor of the mob. Panic-stricken, those in front tried desperately to fight their way back through the crowd. But the pressure from the rear was too great. The rioters in front were lifted bodily and pushed up onto the platform, were driven inexorably up to the muzzles of those deadly accurate guns.

Closer, closer, they came. In a few minutes, Tim knew, he and Diane would be overwhelmed by an avalanche of human flesh—would be grabbed and torn to pieces by these raging maniacs. A few moments more, at best… and then suddenly his gun was empty.

Diane's barked once more, and he saw it droop uselessly in her fingers. Their ammunition was gone; now the end *was* at hand.

But not yet! Frantically, Tim sprang to his feet, using the empty weapon as a bludgeon, hammering and flailing around him until his hands and arms were splashed with blood. That berserk stand was utter madness, the odds a thousand to one against him. Helplessly, he saw the slavering mob flow around him, close in on Diane. He heard her scream, as she tried desperately to fight them off—and then a hundred arms seemed to wrap around him. From every side they imprisoned him, tearing at him, dragging him down, battering him into oblivion.

A thousand stars seemed to burst before his eyes, a great din roared in his ears—and then this was shot through by a strong, compelling voice that rang out above the tumult.

"Let them alone!" it roared. "You hear me—*let them alone!* You down there on the platform—get away from them, or you'll have me to answer to!"

Amazed, the howling mob quieted. Those on the platform hesitated and half-turned, their faces puzzled, inquiring. And then another voice rose from the auditorium.

"It's Sam Spreckels—up there in the balcony!" came a shout of recognition. "They're Operator 5's snoopers, Sam!"

Now every eye was turned to where a slouch-hatted figure stood at the railing in the center of the balcony that ran along three sides of the auditorium. Grimly the man they called Sam Spreckels eyed them, and the effect of his personality began to make itself felt, began to quiet them.

"You two on the platform—the girl and her companion—I want you up here," he commanded in a voice that carried across the big hall. "Make way for them, the rest of you."

Half-supporting Diane, who was dazed and almost unconscious from the mangling she had received, Tim started through the lane that opened for them. He prayed fervently that this luck would hold. Wild exultation welled up within him and new strength seemed to flow through his veins. He knew that voice, could not be mistaken....

But another in that hall knew it also. "That's not Sam Spreckels!" shouted a yellow-shirted New Dawn trooper, who had wormed his way to the front of the balcony. In the same moment he leaped and sent the slouch hat spinning out over the balcony railing. "By God," he roared, "it's Operator 5—in Sam Spreckels' clothes!"

Tim Donovan groaned, but before the mob could grasp what

had happened he had reached the stairway to the balcony, was racing up the steps with Diane at his side. They reached the top without interference, but there the outraged wolf-pack closed in on them.

Desperately Tim plowed into them, madly battling his way toward Jimmy Christopher. Through the fray, he could see Jimmy leap upon the fellow who had unmasked him, loose an uppercut that lifted him from his feet and sent him sailing over the balcony rail. And then Jimmy's gun was out, barking deliberately as it stopped the leaders and held the mob in check.

That was all Tim saw before he went down under the rush. Frantically, he fought back to his knees, but his assailants were far too many for him—no man could stand up under such odds. Then dimly he realized that someone else was standing up there beside him—a man he had never seen before. Tim saw this newcomer's fists do yeoman service, clear a way for Diane, smash two big bruisers out of the way—and give Tim, himself, a chance to get to his feet.

Then, once more, the voice of Jimmy Christopher dominated that close-packed hall.

"Yes, my gun is empty," he echoed a shout that had come up from below him, "but do you see these?" High over his head he held his hands, and in each he gripped what looked like a long metal pineapple. "They are filled with TNT—enough to blow this hall down over your heads and blast you all into mincemeat. I have half a dozen more of them here—grenades you were supposed to use against American soldiers. Unless there is quiet in this hall in ten seconds I'll start letting them fly!"

"You can't get away with that—" someone started to yell, but instantly he was overwhelmed, silenced by his fellows.

"That's Operator 5! He'll do it, you fool!" they cursed him— and in less than the stipulated ten seconds the fear of death had stilled that wild pandemonium.

UNHINDERED, DIANE and Tim walked to the edge of the balcony, but Jimmy Christopher hardly glanced at them. Alertly his eyes scanned every corner of that auditorium, missing nothing as he gave quick orders.

"Take two of these grenades from the bag at my side, Diane," he directed. "I want you to go downstairs and hold the main door. See that nobody leaves here. You, Tim, do the same—you hold the rear door. And if they try to rush you, let them have it!"

Promptly Diane and Tim followed his instructions. Once they were on guard at the doors, none of the terrified New Dawners dared come near them. Then began one of the most remarkable endurance contests of all time. Three people against a thousand. A man, a young woman and a boy scarcely out of his teens—against a thousand drug-maddened huskies.

But behind them the three had half a dozen deadly grenades, and the voice of Jimmy Christopher.

"You are making such a terrible mistake." Jimmy patiently told that smoldering-eyed throng. "You don't realize what you are doing. You don't understand that you are being tricked, used as cat's-paws to betray your country and hand it over to scoundrels who will set up the worst despotism the world has ever seen. That's what you are doing to America and to yourselves!"

At first they howled him down, until the up-raised grenades

warned them to sullen silence. But Jimmy was not discouraged. Again and again, he talked to them as the long hours of the night slipped past. Midnight, and the day of the New Dawn was at hand—but he held them there and talked to them, talked until the persuasive magic of his compelling voice began to have its effect.

Gradually the frenzy of the drug, administered to them in the toast they had drunk, began to wear off. They were listening now, glancing at one another doubtfully, uneasily.

"You are on the verge of treason—treason to yourselves and families as well as to America!" his words dinned into their ears... and as dawn began to streak the sky and gray the auditorium's windows he saw at last that he had won them.

Shamefaced, they were ready to confess their mistake and renounce their allegiance to the New Dawn. Before he was finished, the outbreak—which was to have been a signal and an example for others throughout the nation—was completely thwarted. The arms, which were to have been turned against American soldiers, were reclaimed—and the New Dawn in Pittsburgh was a thing of the past.

Not until then did Operator 5 sit down and rest his weary throat as his newly won friends crowded around him to reaffirm their loyalty.

Poor, misguided tools! Jimmy looked into their ingenuous faces and realized how easily they could be molded to the will of a political trickster; and yet it was with material just such as this that the great wars of the world were fought....

From the crowd abruptly emerged an earnest, intelligent face that was not like the others—a wide-browed, gray-eyed face that looked into Jimmy's keenly, anxiously. He recognized that face. It was the man he had noticed battling at Diane's side in those crucial moments when the mob almost tore her to pieces.

"You don't know me, Operator 5," the man's voice was saying quietly, "but I believe you have been receiving some of my messages. I have been working undercover with this outfit for the past three months because it is the most dangerous threat America has faced since the Purple Invasion. I also wanted to prove to you that I have the qualifications you demand in those who serve you.

"We have only begun to fight against this New Dawn, Operator 5—and I want to go through the rest of the battle with you," he urged earnestly. "This thing is like a huge octopus. Its head is in Europe, and its tentacles are reaching out all over the world. You have chopped off one of them here—but there are many more that are reaching out greedily for the very life of America. While you are freeing Pittsburgh from the toils, New York, Chicago, a dozen American cities—even the capital itself—are being enmeshed and throttled!"

It was in this manner that Operator 5 met Guy DeMott—and out of their meeting were to come the events that produced such a profound effect on the course of American history....

## CHAPTER 3
## A WORLD IMPERILED

A N INTERNATIONAL octopus—that was the picture Guy DeMott drew as he faced the three persons on whom the fate of America so often had depended. A sinister devil-fish whose slimy tentacles were myriad, each one a constant threat to the liberties of mankind—to the very existence of the American nation!

"The American organization is working hand in glove with the New Dawn outfits in Great Britain and France," he finished, his voice quivering with tensity. "They are all under the control of a 'liberator'—a European leader whose identity I was not able to establish."

"Evan Carliotti, the son of a French-Italian father and a Scottish mother," Jimmy Christopher supplied. "One of the most unprincipled adventurers the world has ever known. If he succeeds in seizing control of the French and British governments we will have him on our doorstep. The only way to prevent that is to stop him before he becomes too powerful."

"And that means stopping him in Europe," DeMott nodded agreement. "I was hoping you would reach that decision."

"To kill a devil-fish you must strike at the head, the brain," Jimmy's voice was hard, tight. "That will be a task for a small group of picked men. Men who will work hand in hand with British and French authorities to nip these rebellions in the bud—"

"Men, Jimmy?" Diane Elliot interrupted as she looked at him appealingly. "Can't women share in that work? Can't I—"

Jimmy Christopher's fingers closed over her hand and clasped it affectionately, but he shook his head.

"Not this time, Di," he refused. "This is a job for men—and, besides, we need you here in Pittsburgh. The New Dawn in this area seems to be completely wiped out, but there may still be fire in the embers. We can't afford to let them smolder and break out when our backs are turned. I want you to stay here and keep your eyes open. And that goes for you, too, Tim." He turned to where young Donovan sat eagerly listening. "The task here may be even more important than the one we face in Europe."

For an instant Tim's lips half-opened in protest, and the disappointment was plain in his eyes. But he mastered it and nodded in reluctant acquiescence.

Time was precious if this plan were to succeed, and Jimmy Christopher wasted not a minute. Even before he and Guy DeMott boarded a plane for Washington, his mind was busily considering those who would accompany him. At the airport he dispatched a dozen wires to the likeliest candidates, but his first appointment in Washington was to be with the newly inaugurated President.

It was early afternoon when he drove into the city and announced himself at the rebuilt White House, but to his surprise Andrew Warren was not there to meet him.

"He left nearly half an hour ago," one of Warren's secretaries divulged. "Secretary Hubbard called him from the War Depart-

Suddenly she stiffened in his arms—went limp!

ment. There is some sort of trouble over there—something I would not have mentioned to anyone but you, sir."

THAT SOMETHING was wrong at the War Department was evident the moment Jimmy arrived there. The building was

bristling with guards, but a captain quickly escorted him to the scene of the trouble.

"President Warren was hoping you would arrive, sir," he saluted. "He is with Secretary Hubbard now—in Doctor King's laboratory."

Trouble in Dr. King's laboratory... Jimmy Christopher's brow wrinkled as he quickened his step. Dr. Norman King was one of his warmest friends. A physician who craved a wider field than that offered by private practice, he had realized his ambition when his research work had saved the nation from a threatened plague during the short-lived Mexican-Japanese invasion.* As a result of that distinguished service, he had been installed as head of a research laboratory located in one of the wings of the War Department Building. Here he could follow his chemical and scientific experiments to his heart's content.

Medicine and modern science, it was Norman King's creed, must march arm in arm with munitions and armaments in the defense of America. With that objective, he had gathered around him a corps of brilliant young scientists who were striving to combat the latest efforts of the poison-gas manufacturers of Europe.

His laboratory was Norman King's pride, but Jimmy found one section of it a complete wreck. King, with President Warren and Secretary Calvin Hubbard, were glumly inspecting the charred walls and ruined equipment that seemed to be the aftermath of a raging blaze.

"One of the experiments go wrong, Doc?" Jimmy asked, as the trio turned to greet him.

"Worse than that, Jimmy," King's eyes were dark and raging. "This was no accident—it was murder and arson. Graham Lawrence, one of my best men, died here. His murderers tried to make his death look like an accident—but we have autopsied the body and found that knife wounds had split his heart.

---

* Author's Note: For an account of Dr. Norman King's heroic and spectacular service during the Mexican-Japanese invasion, the reader is referred to "The Day of the Damned."

He was murdered, and then the place was soaked with gasoline and set on fire."

"Why?" Jimmy wanted to know. "What were they after, Doc?"

"That is just what we have been trying to discover," Calvin Hubbard answered. "Doctor King says that Lawrence was conducting a series of special experiments. He was on the track of something he considered extremely important. But he had been reticent about it—and now we probably never will know what it was, for his notes and records have all been destroyed."

Hubbard went on. "How anyone could have gotten in here is as puzzling as the motive for the murder." Hubbard's dark, penetrating eyes darted around the ruined laboratory as if they would find the answer there in the wreckage. "Guards are always on duty at all the doors—and yet none of them saw an intruder coming or going. It almost seems as if Lawrence *must* have done this himself."

On any other day Jimmy Christopher might have been inclined to agree with the secretary. But this was Andrew Warren's inauguration day, the day that was to have signalized the outbreak of the New Dawn—and he could not deny the hunch that this mysterious attack was tied up with the forces against which he was pitted.

"Not a very good omen for the beginning of my administration, is it, Jimmy?" Warren tried to grin wryly when he was closeted with Jimmy in his White House study. "But tell me about Pittsburgh."

Jimmy Christopher told him, and as he listened, Andrew

Warren's sturdy New England face seemed to age, to become haggard.

"One trouble on the heels of another," he commented bitterly. "If I thought that the people did not want me, that it would help for me to get out of office, I would resign—"

"America wants you, sir," Jimmy interrupted. "America needs you now more than at any time since you have been at the head of the government. Our mission in Europe will be a desperate one—but, even if we succeed, our efforts will be useless if the New Dawn agitators get the upper hand here while we are away."

"They won't, Jimmy—not if I can help it," Andrew Warren promised fervently. "Get your men together—and God grant that you arrive in time to wipe out this poisonous infection before it spreads throughout the world. If you stamp it out in Europe, you will be saving thousands—maybe even millions—of lives in America."

FOR NEARLY a week Operator 5 worked at recruiting that little company. Eight men, besides himself, he wanted—four to work in England and four to go to France. Each of them must be a diplomat and an undercover man of unquestioned ability. Each must have a hundred varied talents at his command—and each must be entirely dependable in any emergency.

Eight men out of the hundreds who came in response to his calls…. Carefully, Jimmy picked them. Guy DeMott, whose knowledge of the New Dawn conspiracy made him invaluable. Russell Greene, a veteran of the Suicide Battalion that had once before followed Operator 5 into France. Edward Perry, who had served with him in Mexico. Daniel Harland and Robert Kent, Earl Seeley and Nathan Boone—all perfectly equipped for the task. And then Larry Trowbridge, who for the past year had been one of his most trusted agents.

It was the day after he accepted Larry that another recruit came to his office—a pretty and charming candidate.

"I am Clara Whitney, Operator 5," she told him as she sat nervously beside his desk. "That probably doesn't mean anything to you—but perhaps it will mean something if I tell you that I am going to be Mrs. Larry Trowbridge. That is why I am here—I want to go with him. Please, Operator 5—certainly there must be some way that I can help. Certainly there will be ways in which you can use a woman. I am no tyro at this sort of work—I have been a private investigator."

Eagerly she rushed on, trying to sway him, but Jimmy Christopher shook his head regretfully.

"We are going to be married tonight," she finished her plea. "Surely you won't take him away from me so soon. You *will* let me go—"

But Jimmy could not.

Larry Trowbridge and Clara Whitney were married that night, and two days later he came to the ship to join his mates—alone.

"Clara did not feel up to a shipboard farewell," he grinned an answer to Jimmy's inquiry. "We said our good-byes this morning."

ALERT AND on the lookout for anything that might occur, Jimmy watched the dock until the vessel sailed. Not until they were out of the harbor, and the shore of America faded, did he relax his vigilance. But gradually, as the days passed with nothing untoward happening on board, and no radio reports of trouble in America, he began to feel that perhaps the New Dawn movement had been checked.

Those days dragged interminably, but at last they were only one day out from England. Plymouth in the morning… and then their task would begin!

Standing at the rail with Greene and Kent, Jimmy was on the foredeck, looking out thoughtfully into the thick darkness through which the vessel stole like a grayish, half-seen ghost— when suddenly there was a wild scream from somewhere up near the prow. Jimmy tensed, and heard it again. The frightened scream of a woman!

Before he could more than move from the rail, he saw her rushing across the foredeck, a whitish blur running toward him—that threw itself into his arms and clung to him.

It was the trembling form of Clara Trowbridge!

"I've been below decks—hiding," she half-sobbed. "I stowed away so that I could be near Larry—but I couldn't stay down there any longer. There are other stowaways down there—three men. I've been hiding from them, but tonight I heard their talk, saw what they were doing. They have dynamite or some other terrible explosive—and are going to sink the ship! They saw me, started to run after me! Oh, God—there they are coming now!"

Suddenly, she stiffened—then went limp in his arms. Before Jimmy could catch her she had slipped to the deck—and at that moment orange flashes stabbed out of the darkness in half a dozen places. Bullets whistled by his head, tugged at the back of his coat above the shoulder-blade… and only the fact that he was half-stooped trying to break her fall saved his life.

Instantly Jimmy was down on all fours, revolver in hand. Crouched double, he darted across the deck, returning that fire. Greene and Kent were close at his heels, and now he heard the voices of Seeley and Harland as they came running out on deck.

Jimmy's rush carried him into the thick of the attackers. For a brief instant, he was face to face with one of them, lashed out at the fellow with his gun but missed—then went down as he stumbled across an inert figure. When he scrambled back to his feet, his antagonist was gone—but Jimmy was almost certain that it had been Evan Carliotti!

Like magic those attackers vanished. When a spotlight from the bridge was turned down on the foredeck, it proved empty of all but Jimmy's men—and the still figure that lay face-down on the boards. Curiously Jimmy bent over him, and found that he was a member of the crew—a sailor drilled through the head.

That required explanations. Quickly an officer whom Jimmy recognized as Third Mate Billings appeared with a squad of sailors and closed off the foredeck. He listened to Jimmy's story of an attack by half a dozen men and ordered the ship searched.

But an hour later his men reported no sign whatever of stowaways on board—and no sign of Evan Carliotti.

Skeptically Billings heard Jimmy repeat his story.

"This will be a matter for the authorities in Plymouth," he decided. "Meanwhile I shall have to lock you men in your cabins."

But before he could carry out that intention an orderly appeared with a message. The captain wanted to see Jimmy Christopher in his cabin.

**THERE WAS** no answer when he tapped on the cabin door. Uncertainly Jimmy took the knob, opened the door slightly—to peer in at the purple-faced body that slumped in an easy chair. Captain Austin Fuller was dead, a rope garrote twisted around his neck.

Swiftly Jimmy stepped inside and closed the door behind him. But already he was too late. Footsteps sounded outside the corridor, and the door opened—to frame the startled faces of Third Mate Billings and another officer.

A trap, of course—beautifully timed. Instantly Jimmy saw that there was no use trying to prove his innocence.

With lightning speed a desperate plan took shape in Jimmy's mind. Before the startled officers could make a move toward him, they were staring goggle-eyed, into the muzzle of his revolver.

"Inside, both of you," he clipped. "Lock that door. "That's right. Now take off your uniforms. Shirts and ties, too. You, Billings—strip the captain's bunk. Take those sheets and tear them into strips. Now tie up your friend there."

42

Jimmy Christopher well knew the damning step he was taking. This was adding piracy to the charge of murder—but he could not do otherwise. Carliotti's devilish scheme was too perfectly planned; there would be no loophole in it—and Jimmy could not afford to be thrown into a British jail, perhaps to be incarcerated there weeks and even months before he could prove his innocence. Carliotti had taken desperate measures to eliminate him.

Sweating with fear of this madman, the trembling Billings obeyed; and then submitted to being tied up himself, a gag being jammed between his jaws.

Next, Jimmy turned to the slumped form of the captain and stripped off his uniform. He donned the blue suit himself and then went to work with a compact pocket make-up kit, studying the dead features as he strove to make his own look as much like them as possible. His task completed, and the captain's body dragged into the washroom, he picked up the cabin phone to call the bridge. He ordered that Greene and Kent be sent to him.

Promptly they arrived—and gaped in amazement when they recognized him.

"You are the new officers of this liner," he told them swiftly. "Get into these uniforms, and then go down and bring the others while I take care of things up here. Our only chance is to take command of this ship and keep it until we reach Plymouth."

One by one, the others arrived. With Trowbridge came his wife, wide-eyed and fearful of the trouble she had precipitated. One by one, Jimmy sent for the other officers and each in turn was overpowered, until all eight of his men were uniformed.

"The rest we'll have to take by surprise," he directed as he led the way out to the bridge. "Be sure that none of them gets away—and after that no man other than ourselves is to set foot on the bridge."

It was over in a few moments. The amazed helmsman and navigating officers were overwhelmed and tied up—and from that moment the *Transonia* was under the command of Captain Jimmy Christopher and eight members of the American Secret Service. Throughout the night Jimmy stayed at his post, keeping the liner on its course, while his men guarded the bridge and took charge of anyone whose suspicions seemed to be aroused.

Hour after hour, they kept their vigil, until the sky grayed and the first rays of the sun fell on the steep shore of England. Now there remained only the pilot to be handled, and Jimmy solved that problem at gunpoint once his disguise had lured the man onto the bridge. Helpless, the mariner steered the course to the pier, and the *Transonia* nosed smoothly into her berth.

Amid the cheers of the waiting throng, her pseudo-officers divested themselves of their uniforms—and before the gangplank was lowered they were out on the decks in stewards' uniforms, to mingle with the passengers and slip overside with baggage at the first opportunity. Eight stewards and a stewardess—they made their way out onto the pier and quickly found an opportunity to shed the uniforms which covered their civilian attire.

Last of all came Jimmy Christopher—to stare into the complacently smiling face of Evan Carliotti there among the welcomers! Evan Carliotti, who, only the night before, had been skulking murderously on the foredeck of the *Transonia!* It *couldn't* be....

Before Jimmy could more than gasp at that astounding discovery, he heard the hue and cry behind him. The imprisoned officers must have been discovered. But through the long hours of the night he had made careful plans for this moment—and now he put them to the test.

Shouting excitedly, running after an amazed Britisher who was just leaving the pier, Jimmy sprinted past the surprised customs men and reached the street exit. A cab stood waiting for him. The moment he hopped in beside DeMott and the Trowbridges, the cab got under way. But after them raced two police cars—and the lead that slapped against the back of the cab grimly reminded him that, even though they had escaped Evan Carliotti's carefully spread net, they had leaped from the frying pan into the fire.

Now they were in constant peril. Hunted fugitives, branded as desperate criminals, they would be hounded all over England to face charges of murder and piracy!

## CHAPTER 4
## FIRE FIGHTS FIRE

RUSSELL SQUARE, in London's West End, forbids shops to face the park which is its center. But a discreet little business that does not necessitate altering the residential front of the building—that is another matter. This explains why the agents for Number 72 smiled with approval when the elderly

Hubert Hollingshead inspected the building and decided that it would serve very well for the exclusive antiques showroom he wished to establish. With Hollingshead were his son Cyril and the latter's wife—a refined family who would be a distinct asset to the square.

A few days later, the Hollingsheads moved into the furnished building and cleared the first floor for the antiques which began to arrive shortly thereafter. Nice, genteel people, their neighbors approved—particularly as the antiques showroom seemed to attract very few customers. Gentlemen called at the house occasionally, but for the most part the door remained closed and the place was as quiet as before it was rented.

That was until the night the police raided it.

Hollingshead, senior, was in the little rear room that served him as an office, that evening. He was in conference with his son and two customers who had arrived an hour before. Except for the sound of their low voices the building was as quiet as a tomb—until the office door suddenly swung open and framed Emily Hollingshead's frightened face.

"Police!" she gasped. "There are two of them—outside in the showroom! They want to see you."

But the old man was already on his feet, had reached the door before his companions even got out of their chairs.

"Careful," he warned. "This may be nothing—a routine call. I'll go out with Clara."

And then he was through the doorway, was walking across the showroom, his face mirroring surprised inquiry as his wary eyes sought the constables. There they were, in the front room—

and instantly his keen eyes sensed something wrong. Something about those constables—about that big fellow with the heavy jaw. Somehow he didn't *look* like a constable—and then Jimmy Christopher knew what was wrong!

The fellow's uniform did not fit him! It was too small by at least two sizes—made him look like a rural clodhopper instead of a smart London constable! An impostor in a bobby's uniform....

Every nerve alert, Jimmy strode forward to meet the fellow.

"You wish to see me," he began with a disarming smile—but then his darting eyes glimpsed a heavy shoe protruding ever so slightly from beneath a floor-length drape, saw a telltale shadow against a wall that betrayed where someone was crouching behind a chair.

He understood.

These were no constables! They were thugs in masquerade! Even Carliotti's killers in all probability!

With amazing speed that smiling old man was transformed into a veritable tiger. He hurled himself across the room, and the uppercut which smashed against the big fellow's heavy jaw seemed to be part of the one smooth motion. With a curse, the constable staggered back. Instantly three of his mates leaped out from behind the chairs that had concealed them and flung themselves upon the oldster—flew at him viciously with thick, heavy blackjacks and automatics that clubbed murderously at his head.

Somehow Jimmy managed to spring clear of them—and then he was across the room, dragging the girl behind a sturdy highboy as the constables circled him like hungry wolves. There were six of them now—but out from the office rushed Jimmy's companions. They closed with his attackers in a grim, desperate battle that was ominously silent until one of the constables, knocked backward by a blow to the mouth, went hurtling through a window and out onto the street.

His automatic went off as he fell, and, as if that were a signal, instantly the showroom echoed to half a dozen shots—was ripped and torn by flying lead.

That roaring volley had an immediate effect. It seemed to terrify the constables. Uneasily they darted glances toward the door, started to back in its direction. But now Jimmy's last doubt was removed. He read their intention and promptly moved to thwart it. Lithely, he sprang from behind his barricade—but not quickly enough to elude the arms of the girl who cowered beside him.

"No—no! You'll be killed!" she sobbed, as her arms clasped his right arm and whirled him around, tugged to draw him back.

Death reached out its bony hand for Operator 5 at that moment. Two of the retreating pseudo-constables rallied and took deliberate aim at his defenseless back. Their weapons roared in unison—but not before one of the antique customers had leaped forward and made a human screen of his body. That screen was riven by blasts of lethal lead.

Jimmy Christopher whirled just in time to see the consummation of that gallant sacrifice—Russell Greene pitching lifelessly to the floor. Then he drove two merciless bullets into the hearts of the killers.

Out in front of the building a fresh uproar had started. Vaguely Jimmy heard and identified the sound of squealing brakes, the pound of running feet. Above the uproar, he heard Robert Kent yelling, "They're not cops—they're fakes!" But he already knew that—had positively identified the attackers as impostors before he had cut loose with those unerring deathshots.

Now the real police were arriving. And capture by the police meant exposure of their masquerade—meant arrest and imprisonment on the murder and piracy charges.

"The exit!" he snapped above the tumult.

With a farewell glance at the still body of the faithful companion who had yielded his life so that Operator 5 might live, Jimmy led the way to the rear. In a moment Robert Kent and Larry Trowbridge and his wife were beside him, racing downstairs to the basement, out into the back yard, through a section of the fence they had carefully loosened in preparation for just such flight.

Drawing the loosened boards back in place after them, they were across the adjoining yard, stepping through a lower window of the empty house beyond it, before the newly arrived constables even realized that they had escaped. Once more they had stepped out of a death-trap that had already closed around them. But as they found a cab, and left Russell Square behind, Jimmy Christopher realized bitterly that his every move must have been watched and checkmated. It would be only a question of time before he failed to step out of the fatal clutches with sufficient speed, or when there was no Russ Greene there to ward off the hand of death....

"There are too many of us here," he decided, as the cab bore them across the city to a distant hotel. "Larry, you and Clara will go on to Paris. You will take Ed Perry and Dan Harland with you. Keep me apprised of anything you may discover, and I will join you as soon as our work here is finished."

Before they retired that night, their plans were completed. The four who were bound for Paris would leave in the morning. Bob Kent would go back to Manchester, where he was working in a steel mill. Earl Seeley would stay in Liverpool, where he was employed on the docks. Guy DeMott would go to Birmingham, and Nathan Boone would continue at his job in a London factory—close to the noisome section of squalid Limehouse which was to become Operator 5's headquarters.

CHINESE, PORTUGUESE, Lascars, the dregs of every nationality swarmed in those dismal, close-packed rows of two-story tenements—mingled and intermarried until the polyglot population which resulted was a race apart, a race of narrow-eyed, rat-faced thieves. Of the hundreds of dingy hole-in-the-wall eating places that spotted the district, Ah Lung's Chinese restaurant was the least forbidding.

Ah Lung had a fair trade, not only among Limehouse denizens but with the sight-seeing people who brought tourists to his place. Ah Lung was something of a tourist himself. His periodic absences, when he went on "trips," were well known—so there were no questions asked when Sam Choo, his bland-faced "cousin", appeared in his stead. Business went on as usual, and not even the keenest eyes would have noticed any change in the establishment's shabby clientele—or would have suspected the back-room conferences that sometimes kept Sam Choo awake far into the night.

Those conferences were frequent, for Sam Choo was worried. Try as he would, his very attempt to get in touch with the British Secret Service met with failure.

"I don't know how he manages it, but somehow, I have a hunch, Evan Carliotti has his fine finger in this," he summed up grimly as Bob Kent and Nate Boone, two unshaven, down-at-the-heels workmen, sat in the back room with him. "Twice now we have seen him leaving Sir John's office—and it is more than coincidence that he should have the run of the place while we can't even get Fortescue's ear. Carliotti," he mused, "there's the answer right in front of our faces!"

What he meant became apparent the next morning when Evan Carliotti was announced at the office of Sir John Fortescue....

Sir John looked up from his desk in some surprise as his visitor was ushered into the room.

"Morning, Carliotti," he greeted. "I did not expect to see you today. Thought you were to go—"

The words faded on his lips as he straightened in his chair and

JIMMY
CHRISTOPHER

glanced more keenly at the man who had dropped into the chair beside his desk. His eyes widened in surprise, and his right hand started toward a drawer of his desk—but stopped when he stared into the muzzle of an automatic now trained on his waistcoat.

"No, I am not Evan Carliotti, Sir John," the visitor grinned. "The last time we met, you knew me as Operator 5, of the American Secret Service. But recently it has been impossible for me to reach you. I thought perhaps Carliotti might be more successful."

"Dash it all, Operator 5—" Fortescue frowned—"I have been avoiding you purposely. There are several little matters which now I can no longer evade—the matter of a British seaman murdered, the matter of a British steamship forcibly seized on the high seas, the matter of two men killed in a building on Russell Square—"

"All three of them were matters especially arranged so that you would have to take cognizance of them—all part of a plan to seize world dominion that is now being developed by one of the most unscrupulous rascals you have ever encountered," Jimmy Christopher took up the conversation quickly. And for half an hour he argued, pleaded for understanding, did his utmost to make Fortescue realize the danger that hung over Great Britain as well as over America.

A hard-headed Englishman, Sir John listened and said little. Although his craggy-featured face was almost expressionless, he could not keep the skepticism out of his eyes.

"Rather a fanciful tale, Operator 5—if I do have to say so," he finally observed. "You claim that you fought with Evan Carliotti on the *Transonia* the night the seaman was killed—and yet Carliotti was sitting in this office talking to me at that very time. You say you saw Carliotti in America—and yet I know that he was here in London on the date you claim you encountered him in Pittsburgh."

He frowned. "Those are amazing discrepancies—and yet we have great respect for you here in London. Besides, I realize that frequently in the game we play things turn out to be not at all what they seemed. I can't accept your story as it stands, Operator 5—but I am willing to hold off my men and give you a chance to convince me."

"Fair enough, Sir John," Jimmy agreed promptly. "But I want more than that from you—" and he proceeded to outline the plan on which he was ready to stake the success of his mission, the fate of America, his own freedom—and perhaps life.

IT WAS a week later that Sam Choo sat in his back room and looked into the troubled face of a grizzled ship's engineer who slouched in a chair opposite him. It was nearly eleven o'clock, and the restaurant was almost empty of patrons. Less than half a dozen sat in the outer rooms—and three of those had been in the back room during the past hour.

"There are nearly ten thousand members of the New Dawn in Manchester," the burly steel-worker had reported. "I'm not in the outfit yet, but two of my shop-mates are going to arrange it for me. They have arms and ammunition, everything all set to take over the mills when the word is given. And, from what I've been able to learn, that will be pretty soon."

The engineer's somber face had become even more glum as he

listened to that account. His agitation increased when a disheveled-looking stevedore shuffled through the curtained doorway.

"Things are even worse in Liverpool than we expected, Operator 5," Earl Seeley announced. "The New Dawn has complete control of the dock and shipyard workers. The moment the word is passed every vessel in the harbor will be tied up and maybe seized. That depends on how successful the uprising goes off. If there is opposition, everything will be destroyed—even if they have to level the city. Those were the words of the rabble-rouser I listened to last night."

Manchester and Liverpool—and then London reported, as well.

"You just about have to belong to the New Dawn, if you want to hold a job in the leather factory where I work," Nathan Boone told them when he had his session in the back room. "There isn't any trouble getting in—they drag you in. They brag that it's the same way in every factory in town. There are thousands of them, all planning for the Dawn. No, they haven't any arms yet—but they're all set to take over the arsenals the moment the command is given."

Jimmy Christopher glanced at his watch after Boone had gone. Nearly eleven. Now there remained only Guy DeMott. He should be on hand at any moment—and then the stage would be set.

DeMott arrived on the stroke of eleven. "I've got a job," he nodded an answer to Jimmy's question. "In a knitting mill, a hotbed of New Dawners—"

Jimmy was listening, but his ears were cocked, straining for

55

a sound from the outer rooms—and then he heard it again. The crash of a breaking plate as it hit the floor. Instantly he was on his feet and through the curtained doorway. As he expected, the front room of the establishment was crowded with a dozen evil-looking thugs. They were pressing in, pushing Kent and Seeley back before them, manhandling Boone when he tried to stand in their way.

A yell of triumph went up when the masquerading Sam Choo appeared, and the roughnecks crowded forward, overturning tables and chairs. In a moment the place was in an uproar. Outnumbered, Jimmy's men were retreating, pushed back into the smaller rear dining-room. From his vantage place atop a chair, Jimmy watched them come—watched, and then thrilled with satisfaction.

There at the rear, urging them forward, was Evan Carliotti!

The thugs were almost within reach of his chair when he hopped down and leaped to the side of the room. A moment later and every light except a dismal blue night-night went out. For a moment the rush halted—and then a scared voice shouted a panicky warning.

"Gas!" it clamored. "The blighter—'e's feedin' us gas!"

Now there was no mistake. Choking gas was pouring from half a dozen hose muzzles at various parts of the room. Suddenly protected by gas-masks, Jimmy's men whirled and hurled themselves at the thugs. Choking and gasping for breath, the ruffians had lost all appetite for fighting. Madly they whirled, charging pell-mell for the door through which they had surged into the shop. In utter rout they piled out onto the street, and took to their heels.

"Just as I suspected, Sir John," Operator 5 turned to the ship's engineer when the choking gas had been cleared out of the shop. "They waited until we were all here and then closed in to wipe us out. Now if your men have done their part—"

"They have," Fortescue assured as he came back from the front doorway. "There isn't a sign of the hoodlums on the street, or of my men either. But you can depend on it that they are together and by morning we'll be ready to raid wherever these fellows lead the way."

Jimmy Christopher smiled, but there was grim satisfaction in his heart. His plan had succeeded. Deliberately he had baited Evan Carliotti and his thugs into the restaurant, while Sir John Fortescue's best men, hidden at watching points on the outside, had waited to trail the routed thugs. The plan had succeeded— but its very success confirmed Jimmy's suspicion that there must be a leak somewhere in his own little organization.

Much as he hated to admit it, one of his carefully picked men was a traitor. One of them had passed along to Carliotti word of this meeting tonight—and, so doing, had snared his own crowd by his duplicity. The traitor had failed, but he would be a constant menace until uncovered and disposed of....

**BY MORNING** Jimmy had news of the complete success of his trap. Carliotti's men had been trailed to a warehouse head-quarters, where they had been captured together with an aston-ishing cache of stolen arms and ammunition. Carliotti himself was in prison, and the New Dawn was throttled even before it had been able to raise its head.

A complete victory… but before Jimmy had time to congratulate himself on it a visitor arrived at Sam Choo's restaurant with a message that chilled his satisfaction.

The visitor was Clara Trowbridge, red-eyed and terrified.

"I just got back from France," she gasped. "Oh, God, Operator 5—what I have been through! And my Larry is over there yet! Almost as soon as we landed in France—" she managed to regain control of herself and speak coherently—"we were all arrested and locked up. Not arrested by the police—by these New Dawn people. They took us to Paris and locked us in dungeons way down beneath the level of the streets. I haven't seen Larry or the others since they were taken away from me. But the guard who brought me food and water told me they were going to be executed as soon as the New Dawn came—and that is going to be right away!"

She continued. "I bribed him—with money I had in my stocking—and he helped me to escape. He made it look as if I had knocked him out—but he passed me on to another fellow outside who got me to Boulogne and put me on a boat. It seems I've been days getting to you—I lost all track of time. You've *got* to go back with me, Operator 5. France is on the very brink of a terrible revolution. It will come at any moment, and when it does they will kill Larry!"

When the New Dawn revolution came it would murder not only Larry Trowbridge but the democracies of the world!

Jimmy Christopher's eyes narrowed, as he visualized that

seething menace. He saw his duty clearly. France was like a great volcano, rumbling and groaning on the verge of a cataclysmic eruption. But Evan Carliotti's destructive plotting must be stopped—even if, to do that, Jimmy must walk into the steaming crater, the very heart of that imminent upheaval!

## CHAPTER 5
## START OF A WHIRLWIND

FRANCE WAS in trouble. Jimmy Christopher knew that the moment the London-Paris plane hovered above Le Bourget airport and circled for the landing. Through his glasses he could see that the field was almost deserted—devoid of the myriad of ant-like little men who usually dotted it. When the big transport rolled to a stop, the phenomenon was even more amazing. No dispatcher came out to greet them, no porters, no alighting crew with the portable steps—it was as if the airport had suddenly been completely stripped of all human life.

"Looks as if we'll have to shift for ourselves," the pilot grinned as he and his mate came back into the cabin and opened the door. "Our radio says they're having some sort of trouble here. A strike, it appears to be. Some crowd they call the New Dawn have taken over the field and demand that their own officials be hired in place of the regular staff. Sounds crazy to me!"

The New Dawn... in France the organization had come out of hiding and was brazenly flaunting its strength, making its demands and backing them up with strikes that would be the forerunner of greater violence!

The hour had struck!

Around the operations building Jimmy saw the mob swarming, the black and orange banner waving, and heard the angry shouting of the demonstrators. Time was short now, he knew. When he glanced at Clara Trowbridge, he found her eyes upon him. The same fear was in her mind. She looked at the milling strikers and then shot an uneasy, questioning glance at him. What was he going to do?

Jimmy had talked that over with her already and had made his plans. Those plans depended upon her being able to locate the building where she had been imprisoned. Clara Trowbridge was sure that she could do that... but when they had spent nearly a whole day combing the poorest sections of Paris, without success, she admitted that she was helpless.

"These streets all look the same," she admitted tearfully. "I was *sure* that I could come right back—but now everything looks so different. Oh, however will we find him?"

That was what Jimmy was wondering as he swiftly mapped a new campaign. If the New Dawn outfit was holding his men captive, they might be anywhere in Paris or might even have been taken out of the city since Clara's escape had been discovered. To go to the police probably would be useless—and yet that was the only thing to do. Not to the police but to the French *Surete,* the secret police, who might be keeping tabs on these New Dawners and their various rendezvous.

Besides, it was Paul Challet, head of the *Surete,* with whom he would have to work in Paris.

It was late afternoon before he arrived at the *Surete's* headquarters and started up the wide stone steps of the building—only to stare in astonishment as a man coming down passed him midway in the flight. Jimmy gaped, but there could be no mistake. That man was Evan Carliotti—*who should be behind the bars of an English jail!*

It was incredible, but there the man was. For the fraction of a second, Jimmy had caught a glimpse of his mocking half-smile—as if Carliotti was hugely amused by the baffling game of hide-and-seek he was playing....

Paul Challet rose from his desk and came halfway across his big office to greet Jimmy, the moment he entered. A plump little man with a nearly bald head, he bowed ceremoniously and then regarded his visitor with deep, half-veiled eyes as he pumped his hand.

"Indeed, we in France know of you, *Monsieur le* Operator 5!" he greeted warmly. "It is a rare honor to have you visit us. I shall arrange an audience for you with *Monsieur* Tremel, our president, and I am sure that *Monsieur* Montanye, the premier, will want to talk with you. But first you must allow me the pleasure of entertaining you."

Finally Jimmy managed to break through that flood of conversation and make the man understand that he was not in Paris to be entertained. He quickly sketched an account of the New Dawn activities in America and England, and then reported the disappearance of his men in Paris. But even when he reached this point he could see that the subject made little impression on M. Challet.

"But *Madame* Trowbridge has no idea where this mysterious

TIM DONOVAN

underground prison may be?" The *Surete* director threw out his hands helplessly. "Paris is a large city, my dear Operator 5, and like all large cities we have our thieves. Undoubtedly your friends have fallen into the hands of such a band—apaches, perhaps. If that is so, I doubt very much if they are still alive."

"But this New Dawn outfit—how about them?" Jimmy persisted. "You seem to be doing nothing to curb them. How do you know they do not have a hideout of this sort for detaining their enemies?"

"We are accustomed to political disturbances here in France," Challet said patiently, like a teacher talking to a backward scholar. "We learned long ago that the best method is not to attempt to suppress them but to let them run their course. Always in the end they dwindle away and are forgotten. It will be the same with the New Dawn. It is no different than the others—merely a harmless group of men and women who take their politics too seriously."

And from that complacent indifference nothing could stir him. It was apparent that little help could be expected from the French *Surete*—even though the riotous backwash of the New Dawn was dashing right up against their doors!

The moment Jimmy Christopher started to leave the building he was engulfed in that tempestuous tide....

**FOR AN** instant he stood at the head of the wide steps and stared up the street. The ghastly folly of M. Challet's indifference was driven home to him. There, less than half a block from the *Surete* office, the Rue Brabant was jammed from wall to wall by an oncoming mob—who waved fists in the air and chanted a marching song. The black-and-orange New Dawn flag waved over their heads as they pressed on.

Before that on-rolling tide fell back a half a dozen distressed *gendarmes*, who frantically waved their white batons in a pitifully ineffective attempt to halt the march. Wildly they glanced over their shoulders at the *Surete* building—then almost swooned as another chanting crowd swung into the street from the other direction, closing in on the rear.

Thoroughly frightened now, the *gendarmes* took to their heels, running frantically up the *Surete* steps with the exultant crowd at their heels. Now Jimmy understood why the officers had been turning back so hopefully to the building. Out from behind its doors swarmed nearly a hundred more policemen. With clubs and automatics they charged into the mob—and, before he could step out of the way, Jimmy was in the center of a furious battle.

On every side the struggling forces locked grips and milled desperately. The street was clotted with frantically fighting men, the air filled with clawing fists and flailing clubs. A dozen times Jimmy was hit, knocked down and almost trodden underfoot, as he tried to fight his way free of the mêlée.

Through it all one thought kept flashing through his brain— Paul Challet must have known of this, and yet had given no word of warning. It was possible that the approach of the rioters was a contingency against which precautions were continually maintained—but the thing seemed much more like a deliberately baited trap. Particularly, as it occurred within less than half an hour after Evan Carliotti had left that office.

Suddenly, a vicious-faced brute loomed right in front of Jimmy. In his up-raised hand he clutched a heavy club that would easily have bashed in a man's skull—and when Jimmy stared into his gleaming eyes stark murder leaped out of them unmistakably. *Deliberate* murder, no mere incident of the street battle. Evil triumph leered from them as his club came down—

but in that second Jimmy threw himself backward and the cudgel missed its mark.

Agonizingly it crashed down on his left shoulder and seemed to splinter the bones. But the fierce pain did not stop Jimmy's leap—did not stop his right arm from slipping under the fellow's shoulder and twisting forward. Only a twist of a few inches, but it embodied one of the most effective jiu-jitsu grips—one that Kashawatska Hoia, the Tokyo master, had divulged only to his favorite and most expert pupils.

Like a cork popping out of a bottle, the big fellow shot up out of that swarming crowd, seemed to poise ludicrously over their heads for a long second—then was back in the thick of the swarming mob, going down beneath the battlers with Jimmy Christopher clinging to his throat.

Dozens of feet trod on that silent pair locked in their grim death-struggle—feet that kicked into Jimmy, ground into his ribs, thudded against the side of his head, stunned him. But still his fingers remained locked in that grip. Men tripped and fell over him, tumbled all around him, but still he hung on—until the thing to which he clung was only a limp, lifeless mass of battered flesh....

Groggily Jimmy half-staggered to his feet and stared around him. That desperate struggle had doubly saved his life—not only from the murderous thug he had killed. The tumbled heap of fighters, who had fallen over him, had blocked the tide of struggling humans, turning them back and shifting the center of the battle farther down the street. Around him fallen warriors were picking themselves up, diving back into the fray or edging away to nurse their bruises. A few who lay groaning or white-faced and still.

Right in front of Jimmy was one of these—a young fellow in a yellow shirt with a black-and-orange armband around his sleeve. Blood streamed from a nasty wound above his right temple, the blow that must have knocked him unconscious. One of the New Dawn troopers, Jimmy noted the insignia bars on his shoulder—and then the mob came roaring back as the *gendarmes* drove them in wild rout.

Straight toward the helpless youth they swept. In another moment they would swarm over him, grind him underfoot. But before that could happen Jimmy had him by the shoulders, had hoisted the unconscious body up over his back and was staggering down the street to where he had parked the automobile hired that morning to facilitate the search for his men.

Dropping the youth into the seat beside him, he sprang behind the wheel and started the car... while his moiling brain thrilled to a wild scheme. This youth might prove to be just what he needed—the answer to his problem. At least it was a chance he must take!

Gradually the plan took form, as he worked out the details. He knew that it would succeed. But first he must stop and get to a telephone and reach Clara Trowbridge at the little *pension* where he had left her. He must give her directions for meeting Kent, Seeley, Boone and DeMott when they arrived, instruct her how to carry on until he returned—and what to do in case he was not able to return....

IT WAS two days before the fever left Armand Dupre and he

was able to look around the little bedroom with understanding eyes. Those eyes were now sane but puzzled. Slowly they turned from one unfamiliar object to the other, and finally settled on the face of the blue-bloused Frenchman who came through the doorway and stood looking down at him solicitously.

"Who are you? Why am I here?" came feebly from the pale lips.

"I am Louis Chardeau—and you are here because it takes more than a broken head and a fever to kill you, my friend," the stubbly bearded workman answered. "Do not talk now. Listen, I will tell you. It was three days ago, when you of the New Dawn marched on the *Surete*—remember? There was a riot, and I was swept into the middle of it. I got out just in time to save you from being trampled underfoot by your own friends."

"Yes—now I remember," the injured Dupre recalled slowly. "I was charging the *gendarmes*, closing with a giant of a fellow—and he must have hit me. Then you are not of the New Dawn?" he asked suddenly.

"Not yet," Chardeau muttered grimly. "But after what I saw, the way those cursed *gendarmes* charged upon unarmed workmen—"

Armand Dupre's eyes flashed with approval, and he fell asleep. But when he awoke again he remembered. It was a week before he was able to leave the little cottage on the outskirts of Paris, ten days before he was able to attend a meeting of his committee of the New Dawn—but when he did Louis Chardeau went with him.

Chardeau went along and was hailed as a savior for bringing

Dupre back from the grave. He was accepted as one of them, and listened with glowing eyes as plans for the fast-approaching outbreak were discussed and outlined. What he had suspected was true—all of Paris was seething, a great, human volcano that needed only a spark to set it into terrible eruption....

It was the next morning that Operator 5 appeared at the *Surete,* once more endeavoring to impress upon M. Challet the seriousness of the situation. But M. Challet was very busy—and slightly bored. It was the same with Premier Montanye. He was polite and listened attentively, but he had full confidence in the ability of the *Surete* to cope with the situation—and there was another visitor waiting in the outer office.

They were blind, criminally negligent! While the whirlwind gathered under their very noses, they ignored it and refused to admit that it existed! It was fatuous blindness such as this that cost Louis Sixteenth and Marie Antoinette their heads, Jimmy thought bitterly. Once more the savage Paris mob was working up into a frenzy, getting ready to run amok. But this time the government they would tear to pieces was one of the few remaining props of democracy—a prop that America and the rest of the civilized world could not afford to lose....

Somehow, the blind authorities *must* be awakened to the peril!

THE NEXT night, when Armand Dupre's committee met to receive final instructions from the "Liberator," Operator 5's nerves were atingle. The fatal hour of the "Dawn" was drawing closer—and yet those who were guiding the destinies of France refused to realize what was happening.

Tense and ready for any emergency, Jimmy accompanied Dupre to the meeting—and felt the hair rise at the back of his neck as the "Liberator" entered the meeting room and stood revealed as Evan Carliotti!

Paul Challet had refused to believe that Carliotti had any connection with the New Dawn, had insisted that Jimmy must be mistaken—but here was Carliotti in person. If Challet could be there now he would no longer doubt, could no longer close his eyes to the mounting peril. *He must be brought there!*

The moment he could move his hand to his mouth without being observed, Jimmy gulped the capsule he had brought for an emergency such as this. He pretended to nod with approval, leaning forward as he listened to Evan Carliotti's smooth voice reporting on the state of the movement in the rest of France, and outlining the plans for the seizure of Paris.

The circle of eager-eyed faces was focused on Carliotti. Their voices rumbled approval—and Jimmy's joined with the others. But his tongue was becoming thick and his voice buzzed in his ears. He could feel the blood draining from his cheeks, could feel a wet perspiration coming out on his forehead. He was swaying... and then Dupre was at his side, supporting him and fanning his face.

"You are as white as a sheet," Dupre worried. "You have been working too hard—the excitement is too much for you, Chardeau. It is warm and stuffy in here. You have had enough for tonight. Go home—the cool night air will restore you."

The others voiced quick agreement. They had little time for a sick man—they wanted to listen to Evan Carliotti. Jimmy's legs were shaky as he got to his feet, but he was trembling with elation as Dupre led him out to the door and hailed a cab for him.

In a few minutes he got rid of that cab, and then he was busy at the telephone—calling until he had located Paul Challet and poured his news into the *Surete* director's ear.

"Evan Carliotti—you are sure, Operator 5?" Challet marveled as he listened. "If what you say is so, we have been blind—blind fools in the hands of this master-trickster. But I must see for myself. Where are you, Operator 5? Good… stay just where you are. I will be there within five minutes with a detachment of my men. We will attend to M. Carliotti and the New Dawn!"

At *last* Challet was stirred to action! With a nod of satisfaction, Jimmy Christopher put down the receiver and went outside. He paced the corner restlessly, as he waited for the arrival of the *Surete* men. Five minutes passed—nearly ten. Then two cars drove up to the curb where he stood. Out of one stepped four men, out of the second five others. Paul Challet was in the lead, as they came forward—*came forward with drawn guns and surrounded him!*

"Here is the one," the *Surete* chief identified Jimmy, sharply. "He is the New Dawn agitator who thinks he can now overthrow the Republic of France!" Before Jimmy could more than gasp his utter amazement they were upon him. He was seized, disarmed and dragged to one of the cars. Inside, a gag was jammed into his mouth, when he attempted to protest. Then, helpless under menacing gun muzzles, arms strapped tightly to his sides, he was whirled off into the night....

# CHAPTER 6
# SMOLDERING EMBERS

FOR THE ten days which followed Operator 5's raid on the New Dawn meeting in Pittsburgh—and which had thwarted the Inauguration Day rebellion—peace seemed to settle over America. John Christopher, who took over control of the Washington office, when Jimmy sailed for Europe, now spread a net of reliable agents through the whole affected area. There appeared to be no indication of the smoldering embers against which Jimmy had warned... until the body of Agent Clem Burhenne came floating down the Monongahela sieved by a dozen bullet holes.

Clem had sent in a report of a suspicious gathering near McKeesport. He had promised further details—but what he had discovered would never now be known. When Buck Nagle heard of the killing, he hurried over from Duquesne to investigate—but his automobile unaccountably left the road just outside McKeesport. It crashed into a tree with terrific force, turned over on its side and burst into flames. Nagle was little more than a charred cinder when the local police found the wreckage....

Those were the first of half a dozen agent deaths. Not all were in McKeesport; they were scattered throughout the whole Pittsburgh area.

"These agitators are not finished yet, Diane," Tim Donovan worried, as they sat discussing the mounting death list. "The New Dawn is coming back to life. This time they are being

71

very careful about it. Something is brewing down there in McKeesport—and it's up to us to find out *what.*"

For nearly an hour they considered every possible way of penetrating the town and coming out alive with its secrets. When they had finished, Tim's face was glowing with excitement.

"We only need a dozen of the leaders," he exclaimed, as he started jotting down names on a sheet of paper. "If they meant what they said, and will help us, we can put this over. I'll make the rounds this evening, Di, while you see the police commissioner and anyone else important."

For hours he went from house to house, talking with men who had been in the welfare association hall the night Operator 5 took charge of it—men who had pledged allegiance to Jimmy as the dawn put an end to their incipient rebellion. Wonderingly, they listened to his proposition—and when he was finished, the plans for the revival of the New Dawn in Pittsburgh were complete!

It was nearly a week before those plans materialized. From nowhere the crowd seemed to gather that Saturday afternoon. At first there was only a knot of men. Then several dozen, scores—and in their midst arose yellow-shirted men who harangued them. Magically, New Dawn banners appeared—and suddenly the crowd was moving, resolving itself into a ragged parade that began to sweep toward the center of the city.

But they got little beyond the steel mill district. Here the police took a hand. From every direction they seemed to converge on the demonstrators. So swift was their descent that the fight was over almost before it started. Charging into the crowd on horseback, they broke it up, tore it into bits, pursued the fleeing paraders down side streets in an utter rout.

It was a brief clash, over in a few minutes—but not before the photographers had snapped a dozen shots of the battle; getting excellent pictures of a young, yellow-shirted leader going down beneath a policeman's club, engulfed by a dozen bluecoats. This youth and two others were arrested, held without bail. Yet the moment the cell door closed on him, his pug-nosed face was wreathed in a grin of satisfaction. So far everything had worked beautifully—and the next night the rest of Tim Donovan's plan went off without a hitch.

Anxiously, he eyed his watch until it was ten o'clock. Then he caught the sounds he expected. A low rumble outside, the patter of running feet, men dashing down the cell-block corridor. Now they were at the cell door, unlocking it. Liberated, Tim ran out into the main room of the police station. The officers were helpless under the revolvers of a dozen grim-faced men.

A car, motor running, stood at the curb. Into it leaped Tim and the two companions who had been arrested with him. Quickly, the car darted away, racing down the street as an uproar broke out behind it. Straight through the mill district, they went and then out on the road to McKeesport.

The furious Pittsburgh police telegraphed ahead, but the fugitive car had anticipated that. Twice it whizzed past obstructions that had been hastily erected in its path—was gone before a shot could be fired. And then McKeesport was the next town ahead.

"Now is the test," Tim muttered as he crouched over the

wheel. "The cops in this town are an unknown quantity—but we'll soon know."

The McKeesport police were waiting—half a dozen motorcycle patrolmen who rode out to surround them the moment they came in sight. Tim swerved out of their way, outdistancing them with remarkable ease.

"That means the police are lined up with them," Phil Dugan said softly as he peered through the windshield. "That gesture was only a bluff—here comes the reception committee."

Tim slowed his pace, as the car swung in the direction of the town's largest steel mill. Now cars were converging on them from two sides—cutting them off and then covering them with guns that bristled from the windows. Out stepped hard-eyed men, whose faces broke into grins as they turned their flashlights on Tim and his companions—and compared their faces with the photographs that had appeared in that morning's issue of the Pittsburgh *News*.

"They didn't hold onto you very long, did they, O'Rourke?" the leader chuckled as he shook Tim's hand. "We heard you were on your way here—got a tip from the cops when they heard you were coming. We've been wondering when in hell you fellows in Pittsburgh would come to life."

"We had to lay low—after the way Operator 5 gummed the works for us," Tim grinned. "But we're coming along now. Last night was only the start. There will be more—but we've got to have help."

"Couldn't come to a better place for it," the leader nodded. "The exec committee meets tomorrow night, and you can tell them your story. Follow my car now and we'll fix you up all right for the night."

Tim silently gave thanks, when he stepped back into the car with Dugan and John Allen. He could not have asked for more complete acceptance.

THE NEXT night his luck still held. He and his companions were ushered into the crowded New Dawn meeting, handed cups for the opening toast—which was just what Tim had hoped would happen. With the others, he lifted his drink to his lips. But as some of the heady liquid trickled down his throat, most of it was sucked up by a little hose that he had slipped over the cup's rim. This hose connected with a flat rubber sack palmed in his hand.

Dr. Norman King, back in his Washington laboratory, had been praying for a sample of that liquid!

Then disaster swooped down with startling unexpectedness. Tim's eyes widened, as they settled on a newcomer who had just entered the meeting-room. Slowly, a cold chill trickled down his spine. The new arrival was Hugo Horstman, one of the Pittsburgh leaders who had helped him to stage the mob scene!

Horstman's eyes darted around the room expectantly, searching until they discovered Tim. He licked his lips expectantly. Then dramatically he raised his arm, pointing an accusing finger.

"That fellow is a spy!" he bellowed. "He's one of Operator 5's gang—come here to trick you like they tricked us in Pittsburgh!"

But Tim waited for no more. Like a rocket he leaped from his seat and cleared the distance to the center of the hall. His charge carried him right up to Horstman—and supplied the impetus for the smashing blow he lashed into the informer's face.

Horstman went down. Now Tim was past him, darting toward the door, clearing a way with his fists and the automatic which had suddenly leaped into his hand. Beside him was Allen, doing noble work with the bloodied barrel of his own weapon. After them came Dugan—but he was limping, barely able to keep on his feet, blood bathing his face.

Tim caught sight of his plight and hesitated, started to turn back to help. But Dugan cursed and urged him on, frantically.

"Get out!" he howled above the tumult. "You've got to get clear!"

Even as he spoke, he whirled and threw his long arms around three or four of the foremost pursuers—just as they were about to leap on Tim's back. Dugan's clasp tightened around their knees, spilling them to the floor on top of him. And then John Allen had hold of Tim, was rushing him out of the door, into the cool night air—leading the way in a desperate sprint to where they had left their car.

Back toward the Smoky City they streaked as Allen gripped the wheel, jamming the throttle to the floorboards. Almost immediately the pursuit was hot on their trail. Grimly the chasing cars clung to them, crept closer....

And then their engine coughed!

"Sounds like gas," Allen worried. "We must be low."

His eyes clung to the road ahead of him, as their car whirled around a bend and darted over a straight stretch that clung to the side of a steep hill. Pittsburgh was just ahead now, but the engine… quit altogether!

Frantically, Allen stabbed at the starter, tugged at the choke, trod down on the throttle—without success.

"Hop out and look at the engine, Tim," he called, as he bent low over the dashboard.

Tim sprang out. But before he could lift the hood the engine roared into life, and the car darted away from him. Straight down the road it shot—and then through the side railing with a splintering crash, to pitch and roll sickeningly down the steep hillside!

Finish….

This was no accident, but deliberate! Open-mouthed, Tim stood there and gaped. Then suddenly he flung himself across the road and dived into the brush, wriggled through it until he reached the deep shadow of a low tree—just as the pursuing cars dashed past him. With a shriek of brakes, they drew up at the splintered railing. The pursuers gathered in a knot at the edge of the hill, staring down at the battered wreck now blazing far below.

A painful lump was in Tim's throat as he crept through the bushes on the upper side of the hill. Carefully he circled that group of awed watchers. They knew that they were looking down at ghastly death—but had they realized its real sacrifice their awe would have been tenfold. John Allen, one of Operator 5's trusted men, had died, true to the service that meant more to him than life itself….

"THIS CONCOCTION is a very potent mixture," Dr.

Norman King pronounced, as he completed his analysis of the contents of the rubber sack brought back to Washington by Tim. "It is a combination of drugs, the chief of which is hashish. Its effect is to work the drinker into a frenzy, rendering him extremely receptive to wild, revolutionary ideas. It dulls his sense of caution, completely upsetting his sense of values."

He went on, "A man drinking a cup of this stuff might stay under its influence for eight hours or more. He would be a willing tool in the hands of his masters all during that period. I am quite certain that I can develop an antidote for it, but I'd like to know where they are brewing the stuff. If we could put an end to that, we might go a long way toward paralyzing the whole New Dawn movement."

"Probably they make it there in McKeesport," Tim suggested. "Maybe that is why they guard the place so carefully?"

"Or perhaps they make it in Honesdale," old John Christopher thoughtfully mentioned the name of the small factory town some distance from Pittsburgh. "I have been puzzled about that place. You know the factories there were not altogether destroyed by the Purple armies—they were only half-wrecked. But when we came to reconstruction, it was decided not to rebuild Honesdale. The place was deserted—until recently our men picked up rumors that the factories were operating again."

He frowned. "I sent Dan Hecker to investigate—and that was the last I heard of him. Bill Farris followed him. That was more than two weeks ago, and there hasn't been a word from Farris. But since then I have learned definitely that the Honesdale factories are operating—run by some sort of cooperative crowd who do not welcome visitors."

"The New Dawn!" Tim nodded vigorously.

"Whoever this crowd may be, they are manufacturing something secret—something that it is our business to investigate," the old man said soberly. "One of Secretary Hubbard's men—Henry Pfeiffer, of Military Intelligence—was the latest to try to penetrate the place. That was a week ago. Hubbard is expecting word from him any day, but I fear we've heard the last from Pfeiffer."

"It's the New Dawn," Tim repeated with conviction. "Some more deviltry they're hatching. That was why Jimmy left us out there in Pittsburgh—to watch for developments like that. I'm going back to pay a visit to Honesdale."

"You can't, Tim," Diane Elliot almost pleaded with him. "We agreed, when we came away from Pittsburgh, that your usefulness in that area is finished. You are too well known, and the New Dawn leaders are too anxious to get their hands on you. It would be useless, worse than suicide, for you to go—but there is no reason why I can't find a job in Honesdale."

Tim argued lustily, but Diane was quietly adamant—and John Christopher ruled in her favor.

**THAT WAS** why, three days later, a dusty, shabbily dressed, tired-looking young woman shuffled wearily down the main street of Honesdale and gazed with lackluster eyes at the partially rebuilt town. Curious eyes had stared at her when she came plodding along the rutted road from Meade, and curious eyes followed her as she progressed through the almost deserted streets. But she seemed to take no cognizance of them. Vacantly her gaze traveled from one crumbled building to another—until she spied a store from which the wreckage had been cleared. This store was open for business—a combination grocery and bakery.

With new animation, she hurried up to it, staring longingly through the chicken-wire that served as a windowpane. Hungrily she eyed the food on display, and then seemed to wilt, to slump in a heap as she dropped to the sidewalk....

A dark-haired, square-faced man of about thirty was bending over her when she opened her eyes. His hand reached out, as she tried to rise—pushing her back on the cot on which she lay.

"Malnutrition is her only trouble." He nodded to several keen-eyed men who stood eyeing her with mingled curiosity and suspicion. "I'll warrant she hasn't had a square meal in a couple of weeks—and nothing at all for the last forty-eight hours or more. I'll get her stomach accustomed to food and then blow her to a meal," he chuckled. "I'll take care of her, gentlemen."

He went to the door with them, but when he came back the smile was gone from his face.

"You can sit up now," he said significantly. "They're gone—and *I* know that there is *nothing* whatever the matter with you."

Diane flushed and tried to speak, but he cut her short.

"Time is precious," he clipped. "Let's not waste it. I know you, Diane Elliot—and I'm glad you came. I'm Henry Pfeiffer, Military Intelligence. I managed to get in here ten days ago when they had a bad accident at the factory and needed a physician. That was my chance. I know my pharmacopoeia—army medical—well enough to get by. Since then, I've seen things in this wreck of a town to amaze me—things that Washington ought to know now. But I am watched every minute. Can't get a word out, no matter how I try."

"Hecker and Farris—have you seen anything of them?" Diane asked as she studied him keenly.

"No, and you won't. I know what happened to them," he said with a wry grimace. "They saw too much—and then tried to leave. It doesn't work, but we may be able to work it, you and I."

"How?" Diane was all ears, as she leaned forward and listened while he quickly sketched his plan.

The rebuilt Honesdale factory was in urgent need of workers, and he had little doubt that he could get a job for her there. That would give her an opportunity to learn all that she wanted to know. As soon as she had sufficient information, she would become sick—develop an infectious disease and have to be quarantined.

This would afford her a chance to escape from town.

"I'll have to hold the bag for you here until you return with help—but I ought to be able to keep busybodies out of range for at least a week." He smiled at her eager approval.

HENRY PFEIFFER was as good as his word. The next day he took her to the factory superintendent and got her a job. At first the nature of her employment baffled her. Then gradually she began to understand the peculiar product on which she was working—and the blood ran cold in her veins. This incredible product would make its owners invincible—almost *superhuman!*

This factory—all of Honesdale—was engaged in producing

a weapon such as the world had never seen. It would make the troops of the New Dawn unconquerable. Supermen, they would be able to crush any force sent against them—would march from end to end of America and sound the death-knell of democracy in the Western Hemisphere!

Now she knew what Pfeiffer had meant by his measured words.

Appalled, Diane wanted only to escape from that terrible town. If she could but get back to Washington with news of her discovery and the precious sample now sewed into her clothing! Eagerly, she submitted to the injection Pfeiffer gave her and watched the scary-looking rash that broke out on her skin. Through narrowed eyes, as she lay in bed, she heard him admit to the New Dawn leaders that he had been mistaken in his first diagnosis of her ailment—that she was suffering from an insidious fever certain to ravage all Honesdale once it spread.

Isolated in the little building, near the edge of town where Pfeiffer had quarantined her, she waited for nightfall while she reviewed every detail of the plan. At ten o'clock she would let herself out through the back door, making her way down to the little river that ran through Honesdale. She would follow its bank until she was out of town, and then hurry to the nearest telegraph.

Pfeiffer's life would depend upon her speed, for, once it was discovered that she had escaped, he would quickly share the fate of Hecker and Farris....

At last it was ten o'clock. Diane opened the rear door, stepping out into a dark and almost starless light. For an instant she stood there, her dark cloak blending with the blackness, every nerve tense as her eyes strove to accustom themselves to the Stygian gloom. One step she took forward—and again tensed. This time she knew that her first hunch had been right. Others were close by; she was being watched! Dark figures were closing in on her!

In his eagerness to reach her, one of them stumbled, sprawled headlong. There was a curse in the dark, a rush of bodies— but before they could reach her she was back inside, the door slammed. Hurling themselves against it, they pounded with heavy clubs. The door was giving way, and Diane knew that the plan had failed dismally. Pfeiffer must have been suspected, might already have been apprehended… and now they were closing in to seize her.

This was the end, but one more card was still hers to play. One trick that she had not divulged even to Pfeiffer because she had pledged herself to reveal it to nobody.

The door was splintering, crashing in ward. Heavy feet were leaping over it to pound over the lower floor, as she raced upstairs and climbed out onto the roof.

Fumbling in her eagerness, she tore loose a tube that was strapped to her leg just above the knee—a tube an inch thick and nearly a foot long. Propping it up against a battered cornice, she applied a match to it.

Then the bright glow of the magnesium flare blazed out over the half-skeleton buildings of Honesdale.

Desperately Diane fought to keep her pursuers down under the roof trap, but she knew that her struggle was useless. They lifted the trap and her bodily, surged up through the opening and overpowered her. They kicked over the flare, ground it out beneath their heels—but not before it should have carried its message to where Tim Donovan watched in the brush outside of town. It told him that she, like the rest, had failed....

It was the terrible extent of her failure that wrung a groan of pure agony from her, as they dragged her downstairs. Here, in her grasp, she held the secret that would enable America to combat this growing menace arising within its borders. But now those devilish factories would go on, unhampered, grinding out the incredible sinews of invincibility.

America was doomed....

**THAT SAME** dread thought was mirrored on the faces of the four men who gathered in President Warren's private office, when Tim Donovan got back to Washington and hurried to report to the Chief Executive.

"We could send troops, even by air—but that would doom Diane," Andrew Warren debated, as his pencil worried holes in his desk pad. "They would kill her before we could reach her. Besides, that might give these traitors just the warning they need—give them an opportunity to destroy whatever equipment they may have there. We don't want them to do that. We must know what they plan, what they are trying to hide."

"That is what my best men have been striving to discover," John Christopher admitted grimly.

"And they have failed," Calvin Hubbard added. "Failed just as my man Pfeiffer must have. The place seems impregnable."

For a moment the Secretary of War was silent as he eyed his

chief meditatively, and then he spoke again—slowly, like a man who thinks aloud and listens to the sound of his own words.

"The only man who might cope with this situation is Operator 5," he pronounced, "and he is somewhere in Europe—God only knows where. If only there was some way of reaching him!"

## CHAPTER 7
## THE DEVIL'S "LIBERATION"

**P**AUL CHALLET had betrayed him, had deliberately pointed him out and charged him with being a New Dawn agitator! Jimmy Christopher knew that there could be no mistake. He had identified himself too thoroughly to the *Surete* chief—had even telephoned him and offered to lead him to the New Dawn headquarters. That could mean but one thing— Challet, the head of the French *Surete,* was in league with the New Dawn! He was in league with Evan Carliotti in this infamous plot to overthrow the French government and then sweep on to domination of the entire world!

Faced with the necessity for raiding his own co-plotters, Challet had had no choice but to show his colors. But these men who had seized Jimmy, who held him there in the speeding car—were they renegades also? Or had Challet tricked them as he had tricked the French authorities?

Jimmy had no way of knowing. When he had tried to protest, they had gagged him securely, and now they were watching him as if he were a desperate criminal. It was useless to try to make them listen here in the car. But when the machine stopped, and they forced him out, to drag him into a grimy stone building that stood on the bank of the Seine, he cast about frantically for an opportunity. Unresisting, he walked through the low, vaulted door and through a large outer room where several *Surete* agents stared at him closely. Past them, he went through a damp tunnel, that led into the musty corridor of an ancient jail—and there at last he managed to grind his teeth through the gag, spit it from his mouth.

"You are being tricked, my friends!" he shouted, as he whirled on his captors. "Challet is a traitor. He is deceiving you to protect the New Dawn conspirators who are his fellows—"

But they leaped upon him and dragged him into a solitary cell. Here he was invited to shout his lies to his heart's content.

As Jimmy sank down on the hard cot, and listened to the sound of their retreating footsteps, it seemed to spell the end of everything. Locked up here in this dungeon cell, he would only gnash his teeth futilely while the New Deal rose and sealed the doom of unsuspecting France. Even Carliotti and his fellow conspirators had been so close, within his very grasp—then in the wink of an eye all his work had been undone by the treachery of one of France's trusted guardians....

For three days Jimmy tried vainly to win help from the guards who brought him food and water—to get word to the American ambassador or even to the French premier. But they laughed and tore up the notes he begged them to deliver. Three long days, and he realized that he was a lost man—buried alive, to rot here until his captors were ready to dispose of him.

On the fourth day two of the *Surete* agents came to his cell, instead of the regular guards. One look showed Jimmy that they were greatly excited. It was fear flickering in their eyes.

Wonderingly he accompanied them to the big reception room of the prison—out from that damp, cold dungeon and back into the world. Jimmy blinked as the unaccustomed light stabbed at his eyes—and then a wild flood of sound dinned into his ears. Howls and yells, the frenzied shouting of a great mob, echoed by the thudding of blows against the building, by the roar of shots!

Now he saw that the doors were bolted, that heavy metal inner doors had been closed and securely fastened. Windows were fastened with metal shutters, pierced only by a slit through which the watchers crouched behind them could fire… on the mob now swarming outside the jail!

Now there could be no mistaking the savage clamor outside the building. The New Dawn mob had risen!

"Yes, they are out there," one of the *Surete* men gritted, as his keen eyes watched Jimmy's face. "They have come to rescue you—but they will not succeed. You are going to call off your dogs, *Monsieur* Chardeau, or whatever your name may be. We shall open one of the windows, and you will call out to them to disperse, if they value your life. If you give any other orders—" His automatic raised significantly at Jimmy's heart.

"But you are mistaken, don't you understand?" Jimmy tried earnestly to convince them. "I have nothing to do with the New Dawn. I am an American undercover agent—Operator 5. I was investigating the New Dawn here—was about to deliver them into your hands—when *Monsieur* Challet betrayed me. I have no influence with that crowd. My very appearance there at your window will start them clamoring for my blood."

Now the building was trembling, reverberating to the boom of terrific explosions, and the howl of the mob outside became louder, more savagely triumphant. Thunderously, they pounded on the doors.

"Liar!" the *Surete* agent spat. *"Monsieur* Challet prepared us for your protestations, but they will do you no good. Your friends may tear this building down stone from stone—but you and the rest of your American trouble-makers will be dead before then. Henri," he ordered a trembling guard, "go and bring the others. Perhaps they will be able to convince this one of his folly."

Jimmy's muscles tensed for a leap, but the fellow's finger did not relax on the trigger, and there were a dozen other drawn guns in the room. Penned up there in that doomed jail, the *Surete* men were desperate, on hair-trigger. The first attempt at resistance would mean his death, and yet he might have to risk that chance at any moment....

For what seemed an age a deathly silence held there inside the besieged jail—a palpitating silence in strange contrast to the muffled uproar outside. Jimmy could hear the very breathing of his excited captors. The sound of footsteps coming back along the jail corridor was amplified a dozen times.

But suddenly it was blotted out by another terrific crash—and echoed by a great roaring and groaning as part of the grim stone building must have collapsed. Startled eyes flashed to the doors and windows—and at that moment silent figures leaped from the jail corridor doorway and sprang on the *Surete* men.

Jail guards—but they were led by Larry Trowbridge and Ed Perry and Daniel Harland!

"You will not kill these men and doom us all," one of the terrified guards screamed, as he beat one of Challet's agents to the floor with his gun barrel. "Fools—we will all be killed by their friends if one of these men dies! Open the doors! Let them in!" LIKE A flash, understanding of that strange situation came to Jimmy Christopher—and his fist crashed against his captor's jaws as the agent's automatic blazed. That bullet nicked Jimmy in the shoulder, but in the next second he had the agent's automatic, was using it as a club to beat the rest of the *Surete* men into submission.

So these jail guards, and apparently the *Surete* men as well, did not know that he and his men were not New Dawn leaders! That meant that Paul Challet had tricked them… but this time he had out-tricked himself. Believing that the prisoners would be influential with the mob, the terrified jailers had released them before they could be killed as Challet planned.

Grimly Jimmy promised himself that the *Surete* chief should pay for that duplicity. But now the problem of self-preservation was foremost. Once those doors were opened, the mob would come pouring in—and that probably would mean recognition and quick death for himself and his men. There was one way in which that might be prevented.

"The men in the cells—release them!" he shouted to his friends, as he backed against the door and held the frenzied guards at bay.

Trowbridge and Harland got the idea at once. They raced

back into the cell rows while he and Perry tried to reason with the guards. Only for a few minutes—and then the big room was swarming with released prisoners. Inside the jail rose a clamor equaling that outside. It became a howling panic when the building trembled again and reverberated with the thunder of its own collapsing.

The wall behind Ed Perry cracked from floor to ceiling, stones and cement came raining down… and then the door popped in with the roar of a cannon. With a rush the frenzied crowd poured in, to fall upon the luckless guards and tear them to pieces in the wild carnage that followed.

The only cool heads in that victory-maddened throng, Jimmy and his men managed to keep together, managed to mingle with the mob and lose themselves in it. They met again outside the jail when the ancient building toppled and crushed hundreds of its destroyers as it settled in a whirling cloud of dust.

"They are like a pack of mad, blood-lusting wolves," Jimmy groaned, as he watched the mob dragging the mangled bodies of the prison guards and *Surete* men in triumph through the streets. "Unless they are stopped immediately, Paris is doomed!"

But it was already too late to stop them. Not only this mob, but dozens of others roamed the streets of the French capital, pillaging and wantonly destroying everything in their path. A dozen times that day Jimmy and his men lined up with the hard-pressed police and tried to stem the rioting, but the mob was not to be curbed. A score of times he and his men risked their lives to save luckless victims from the bands of thieves already roaming the streets unhindered.

Exhausted and suffering from numerous wounds, they stood that night in a great city that had been turned into an Inferno. Wherever they looked, the shattered windows of looted stores gaped darkly; wherever they turned, savage mobs of men and women, little better than beasts, roamed the streets, slavering for loot and for victims. The voice of Paris had become a bestial howl—and above the doomed city the sky was crimsoned by the flames now sweeping unchecked from quarter to quarter.

In a day France had been plunged backward more than a century and a half, to find itself in the grip of a mob whose horrible excesses rivaled even those of the First Revolution. But this time, Jimmy realized, there was a diabolically cunning brain directing the Reign of Terror—a hell-spawned schemer who planned to use this victory in France as a springboard for his campaign of world domination.

"The New Dawn," Jimmy muttered, as he turned horror-tired eyes away from the outrages that greeted him on every side. "This is the 'liberation' Carliotti promised them—and this is what he and his gang plan to duplicate in our American cities! There is only one way to stop that," he finished grimly, "and that is to stop Carliotti. We must reach him and put an end to his devilish career before he becomes too powerful—before his bloody fist has a chance to reach out for the throat of America!"

BUT TO reach Evan Carliotti became more and more nearly impossible in the red days that followed. The blaze that had been started in Paris spread like wildfire. From end to end of France it leaped and joined forces with a dozen other blazes that leaped to meet it. And as the fiery destruction swept onward,

Evan Carliotti's power increased… until all of France lay in the palm of his hand.

Under the shadow of that hand, France was blighted, ruined and thrust back into semi-barbarism. From border to border, the land was roamed by vulture bands whose only idea seemed to be to destroy—bands which Evan Carliotti's troopers made no attempt to curb because it was on such as these that his evil power rested….

The day after the outbreak of the New Dawn rebellion, Jimmy and his men combed the wreckage of Paris for Clara Trowbridge and the four who should have joined her from England. The *pension* at which she had been staying, when Jimmy last spoke to her, was now a fire-gutted ruin. She seemed to have been hopelessly swept away by that holocaust.

It was Larry Trowbridge who discovered the clue that located her. Standing in front of the ruins of the *Le Temps* office with the others, he suddenly drew close to one of the bulletin boards on which the New Dawn council was now posting its notices and proclamations. Scribbled in pencil on one side of the sheet was a cabalistic notation—in Clara's script!

That notation took them to the rubbish-littered canyon that had been the Rue Danou, through the wrecked entrance of Number 66 and into the courtyard beyond—where the rear building was still in fair condition. Out from that building came Clara Trowbridge, to throw herself in her husband's arms in a paroxysm of relief; and after her came Kent and Seeley and Boone. Guy DeMott alone was missing.

"Guy is the reason we are enjoying these sumptuous quarters,"

Bob Kent explained his absence. "He is one of the big shots on the Paris executive council, and this place is under the protection of the New Dawn."

"Which makes it the finest possible location for our headquarters," Jimmy Christopher decided promptly. "It is the last place in which they will look for us—and from here we may be able to scent the trail that leads right to Evan Carliotti." Without delay he planned his campaign and assigned his men their roles. To reach Carliotti was their goal, and each of the eight used his own methods and approach to locate the revolutionist chieftain. For a week they worked, eight Americans who outwardly were now as French as any Parisian—and gradually they began to insinuate themselves into the New Dawn organization.

But that progress was slow, and the destructive progress of the rebellion was appallingly swift. President Tremel and Premier Montanye had tried desperately to stem the uprising, but when the very troops on whom they counted had pinned New Dawn armbands on their sleeves, they had been helpless. Seized by the mob, they were hooted and stoned as they were dragged off to prison.

Here and there some local official managed to stem the tide for a few days, but one by one they were slain or thrown into jail. Day by day the bulletins which came back to Jimmy's impromptu office were more and more disheartening. Day by day the radical elements of the New Dawn seized more power and the list of the dead mounted higher and higher—until it seemed that the bloody guillotines, that had been erected in the

His hand darted from his pocket—and
now held a crashing automatic!

Place de la Concorde, must collapse beneath the steady stream of victims marching up.

"Blood, blood—all they think of is blood!" Jimmy groaned as the cream of France's population joined in the grisly death-march.

Strangely, Tremel and Montanye had been spared, but at last the long-expected notice was posted on the council's bulletin

board. President Tremel and Premier Montanye had been tried by the revolutionary high court and condemned to death. They would be executed at noon the next day.

Heartsick and helpless in the face of this wanton slaughter, Jimmy Christopher trudged back to the ruins of 66 Rue Danou at the end of a discouraging day. Tremel and Montanye were only two men, but their execution would have a vital signifi-cance.

It would wipe out the last vestige of the old order and estab-lish the New Dawn without a rival as the governing body of France. It would bring that much nearer the day when Carliotti was ready to turn his eyes to America....

BUT THE moment Jimmy climbed down to the basement room, that served him as an office, he saw that the grim specter of tragedy had come even closer than he realized. Clara Trow-bridge was waiting for him there, her eyes red with weeping, a bit of rumpled paper clutched in her hands.

"I knew something had gone wrong when we didn't hear from Larry last night," she sobbed. "They have caught him, Operator 5! They have condemned him to the guillotine!"

From her fingers Jimmy took the note and spread it on the table before him. There it was, in Larry's handwriting, a brief farewell that he had managed to smuggle out of prison.

"Perhaps this is a trick," Jimmy tried to console her. "Perhaps it is a forgery intended to trap us—"

But even before the words were out of his mouth they were irrefutably answered when the door opened and framed the figure of a yellow-shirted New Dawn trooper. A patch covered his right eye, a droopy mustache hung from his lip and he wore his hair long and straggly—but there was no mistaking Guy DeMott, now of the Paris executive committee.

"You've heard, I see," he said quietly as he dropped into a chair and looked from Jimmy to Clara Trowbridge. "I haven't had a chance to get to you sooner—shouldn't be here now—but I wanted you to know. There isn't a thing I or anyone else can do. Carliotti is the only man who could set aside that sentence."

He went on. "This isn't just an ordinary, run-of-the-mill condemnation—it's high treason. Larry waylaid Ladue, of the executive committee—took his clothes and papers and managed to get into the St. Denis prison to see Tremel and Montanye. He had some desperate scheme for helping them to escape—but the guards grabbed him in the middle of it. That gave Carliotti just the excuse he needed for executing the president and the premier. Larry is going to the guillotine with them. There is a double guard outside their cells now, and all of Paris will be there tomorrow."

Clara Trowbridge's heartbroken sob stopped him, and he looked at her pityingly, then started to speak again. But now she was sitting up, her jaw firm, her eyes flashing.

"There are seven of you here—seven of America's most resourceful secret-service men—and you intend to stand by without raising a hand while Larry is murdered before your eyes! I thought you were men."

"Larry will not die on the guillotine," Jimmy Christopher said softly, and the peculiar matter-of-fact tone of his voice stopped her, choked her hysterical outburst. "We still have almost sixteen hours to complete our plans for his rescue."

"You *couldn't* do that!" DeMott gasped impulsively. "You wouldn't have a chance…." But something in the depth of Jimmy's eyes stopped him, made him hesitate. "By Jove!" he almost whispered. "There might be a chance at that, a chance in a million—"

"One chance is all we need," Jimmy reminded, "and when we pull Larry out of the fire we will be giving Evan Carliotti the first punch that leads to the knock-out!"

## CHAPTER 8
## WOLVES' DAY

B Y EARLY morning the Place de la Concorde was crowded, and long before noon feverish-eyed human-ity packed it from side to side. Looking down at that savage, unkempt throng, one might well have supposed the date to be the Eighteenth Century instead of the Twentieth. Just such a mob as this had howled for the heads of their rulers in 1793; just such wild-eyed men and women had cackled their delight every time the sharp blade of the guillotine sheered off another luckless head. At that time they wore red caps and badges; now they sported dirty yellow shirts and armbands. But beneath the outer symbols they were the same rapacious wolves come to glut their appetite for human blood and misery.

All morning the steady stream of condemned victims had flowed up to the three hard-working execution machines. But these lesser performers had received scant attention. It was the president and the premier of France for whom this milling audience waited so impatiently.

By eleven-thirty the procession of the lesser victims ended, the better to set the stage for the main event. It was a quarter to twelve when the dignitaries of the high court and the Paris executive committee took their places on the high grandstand erected near the main, central guillotine. The bloody-handed lords of the New Dawn—with Evan Carliotti smiling complacently in their midst!

The crowd fidgeted, mumbled—and then was hushed as a black-robed priest wended his way through the open lane and mounted the platform. The round, wide-brimmed hat of his order pulled down well over his bowed head, he seemed hardly aware of the dense crowd that surrounded him on every side as he silently fingered his beads.

The giant figure of the executioner moved to its place. The pompous clerk with the death warrants cleared his throat so that his part in the grisly drama should be perfect. Then a ripple of excitement swelled into a wave, a roar of sound sweeping over the square. The condemned were approaching! Out there at the far edge of the crowd the tumbrel had come in sight. Instead of the jolting, two-wheeled cart of bygone centuries, the modern death conveyance was a large open motor-truck, its side-poles capped with the ghastly heads of some of its recent passengers!

Hands tied behind them, their backs lashed against a spar that had been set up in the center of the truck's floor, stood President Pierre Tremel and Premier Georges Montanye—accompanied by Larry Trowbridge, the man who had tried to liberate them. Unafraid, they looked out over that sea of faces, ignoring the smugly grinning countenance of Paul Challet, who sat with two other guards at the rear of the vehicle.

The savage roar swelled to ear-splitting proportions as the truck reached the guillotine and came to a stop. Challet's men lowered the tailboard while he stepped up to the prisoners and began to unfasten them.

The president first…. A hush fell over the gaping spectators as Pierre Tremel started toward the rear of the truck. The priest walked to the edge of the scaffold and stood at the top of the steps to receive him. For a split-second that was the tableau— then things began to happen so swiftly that no two of the thousands of eye-witnesses ever were able to agree on exactly what did happen.

Suddenly the priest dropped his beads. His finger pointed down at the death-truck, pointed squarely at Paul Challet— and then spouted flame. Challet pirouetted as his knees corkscrewed beneath him, turning in an almost complete circle—as if to show all that vast audience the blood-spouting hole that had blossomed in the center of his forehead!

The stunning surprise of that shot held them momentarily transfixed. Before anyone could interfere, the priest's hands darted beneath his robe, flashed out again and hurled something high in the air—something that landed in the thick of the mob and exploded with a terrific crash. Another object arced over the mob on the other side of the scaffold and exploded in the midst of the terror-stricken throng now desperately trying to fight their way clear.

In the same flashing half-second that the priest's gun roared and his hands disappeared beneath his robe, men sprang from nowhere, from everywhere—half a dozen men who seemed to be the only ones in that packed square who knew what to do. One sprang up on the platform beside the black robe, was smashing the gaping-mouthed death-warrant reader over the head with an automatic barrel, then emptying its bullets into the chest of the onrushing executioner.

Another man was on the step of the truck, clambering into its cab, to quickly subdue the surprised driver. Only a few seconds of deadly struggle, then the driver's body toppled overside as the victor slipped into his seat behind the wheel.

Other men slammed the truck's tailboard back in place, sprang up beside the condemned men and poured a scorching hail of lead into those who stood nearest to the machine. That hail of death cleared a way for the truck, as the new driver threw it into gear.

"Stay where you are—all of you!" the voice of the priest bellowed over the square. "I have plenty more of those grenades, and the first man who tries to stop that truck will get one!"

For a moment it seemed that his threat had cowed them, and that no man would dare to disobey. The truck was underway, starting through the crowd... and then the spell snapped. With an outraged roar, the mob started to close in—the cringing ones nearest the scaffold driven on by those pressing up from behind. And at that moment the New Dawn troopers, who had been holding back the crowd, came to their senses. Shots began to roar, and bullets spattered against the scaffold, ricocheted from the gleaming blade of the guillotine. Howling like maniacs, the mob rushed for the death-truck, closed in on it, and tried to block its way—then suddenly the machine seemed to catch fire. Clouds of thick smoke billowed out from beneath it—heavy gas that spread out on all sides and threw the attackers back, coughing and gasping.

Tensely Operator 5 watched… and breathed a sigh of relief when he saw that the stratagem had worked. The truck was free now, cutting its way out of the square. Ed Perry stiffened for an instant on its edge and then pitched overside, and Nathan Boone followed him—to be seized and torn to pieces horribly by the enraged mob. But Bob Kent, in the driver's seat, was in the clear and speeding his rescued passengers to safety.

OPERATOR 5 heaved a sigh of relief, and turned to the business of saving his own life. So far his wildly impossible plan had worked surprisingly. Earl Seeley, working in one of the New Dawn arsenals; Dan Harland, worming his way into the confidence of one of the mechanics at the garage where the death-car was stored; Bob Kent, Ed Perry, Nate Boone—each had performed his part admirably. Now only Guy DeMott's part remained.

Crouching low on the scaffold beside Harland, Jimmy peered over the edge of the bullet-pocked wooden railing—then blasting lead carried away his priest's hat. The mob was closing in, rushing the guillotine, and still there was no sign of Guy.

Jimmy Christopher's jaws clenched, his eyes hardening. Those two grenades he had thrown into the mob were blanks, loud detonators that would do little harm. But now was no time for such niceties. Over the railing he hurled a handful of sudden death—another, another.

Screams of agony echoed the detonations, and that wild rush for the guillotine stopped. It hung back until Evan Carliotti, leaning out of the grandstand, urged them on. Again Jimmy's arm arched, and this time the deadly grenade hurtled toward the stand, striking one end. It dissolved into a mass of splintered wood and mangled humans, but the hit had been too far from Carliotti. He had only been knocked backward by the explosion, and now was on his feet, scrambling frantically to safety.

There were only two grenades left. Jimmy hurled one, then leaped across the scaffold to where Dan Harland had gone down, his throat almost torn out by a bullet. That made three lives that had been paid for the three snatched from the guillotine's hungry blade. In another few seconds, the price would be four....

But at that moment Guy DeMott came through!

Knifing its way through the mob, came an armored car. Attached to its sides and wheels were long, gleaming-bladed knives that carved a way for it without even wetting its sharp edges. Straight up to the guillotine it roared, and then the back door opened. Out poured half a dozen yellow-shirted troopers—the loyal Frenchmen Guy had enlisted for this desperate attempt!

Jimmy was already down the steps, sprinting toward the open door, to be seized and dragged inside. The others jumped in after him, the door clanged shut, and the car was once more under way. Then Jimmy saw, by the pale light of an overhead lamp, that Guy DeMott was not in the car. He, himself, was being covered by gun muzzles from every side. These men searched him, taking his automatic and the last of the grenades.

This was not the rescue squad, but *real* New Dawn troopers! Something had gone wrong—very wrong. And as Jimmy sat there reconstructing the details of the past sixteen hours he realized, as he had in London, that somewhere there was a leak in his organization. One of his trusted few was a traitor!

It was Guy DeMott. He alone had failed to carry out his assignment. Only DeMott had known where that armored truck was to be seized and prepared for its dash across the square. He had known every detail of the rescue plan—which these New Dawn troopers had carried out on schedule! Guy DeMott was the man who had arrived at the Chinese restaurant in Limehouse just before Evan Carliotti's men swarmed into the place… the one aide about whom Jimmy knew very little prior to their meeting in the Pittsburgh gathering of the New Dawn plotters….

By the time Jimmy had arrived at this reluctant conclusion, the armored car had stopped. He was taken into the massive Luxembourg Palace, which had been taken over by the New Dawn leaders for a combination headquarters and courthouse. Straight to the basement his captors dragged him and locked him in a cell….

IN LESS than half an hour a squad of yellow-shirred troopers came for him and led him up to the big salon where the high court was in session, Evan Carliotti presided as its chief magistrate. The trial was a farce, a travesty of justice. Charged with plotting to overthrow the established government of France, of aiding in the escape of its condemned enemies, and of making an attempt against the life of its liberator—Jimmy's conviction was a foregone conclusion. When Carliotti pronounced the death sentence, Jimmy understood why the New Dawn troopers had bothered to rescue him instead of letting the mob tear him to pieces.

"Operator 5, this high court has found you guilty of three major crimes, any one of which makes the imposition of the death penalty mandatory," Carliotti glowered. "For that I sentence you to be executed on the guillotine tomorrow at high noon. But your death alone will not satisfy these outrageous crimes. You, the foremost secret-service agent of a foreign power, came here in your official capacity to overthrow the constituted government of France. For that we hold the United States of America responsible—and for that, in our time, we will exact complete satisfaction!"

Now Evan Carliotti had the excuse he needed for a war against America! First would come an undercover campaign of revolutionary activity, and when that was at its full height Carliotti would step in and insure its success—with the troops of New Dawn France if necessary. Guy DeMott had indeed betrayed his country completely....

Back in his underground cell, Jimmy counted the hours before the next noon. This time the guillotine would be guarded so that it would be hopeless suicide for any but the New Dawn legions to approach it. There would be none to set aside the sentence of that devil's court.

As Jimmy Christopher stared thoughtfully at the ring on the third finger of his left hand, the turnkey unlocked the cell door.

Jimmy received a profound shock when he glimpsed the face of the guard—Guy DeMott!

"This will be nip and tuck," DeMott clipped. "We have only a few minutes at best, and we'll need all the luck a man ever had. Here—" he tugged a dirty uniform from beneath his long blue blouse-coat—"get into this. I took it from the guard's room when I locked him in. But he'll be found at any moment, and then they'll be down around our ears."

"How did you manage to get here?" Jimmy wanted to know as he fairly leaped into the clothing.

"That's a long story," DeMott whispered, as he watched the corridor anxiously. "Somehow they learned about the armored car—knew just where to go and when. We were blasted down when we tried to take it. They killed the others—eight of them— shot them down at the first volley. But I managed to leap back around the door and escape before they knew that I wasn't among the corpses."

He went on. "I heard about what happened in the square and followed you here. There is a net out for me by this time, of course, but the word hasn't had time to get around to everyone. I gambled on that—walked in and overpowered the unsuspecting guard before he knew what was happening to him. But the moment they know I am in here, they will close this palace so tight that a flea couldn't get out."

106

Jimmy listened to his words and wondered what lay behind them. DeMott's story did not ring true—it was full of holes and did not answer a lot of vital questions. But what could be gained by this attempt to deliver him from his cell? To have him shot down while attempting to escape? But he was to be executed the next day anyway....

Wondering, he followed DeMott down the gloomy corridor and then cautiously up to the main floor of the palace.

At this hour the palace seemed to be fairly deserted. Twice they passed groups of men, but these seemingly were too busy with their own affairs to take notice of two shabby guards who happened to be passing. DeMott's eyes swiveled constantly from point to point. Was he ready for trouble—or looking for the attack he expected? Jimmy wondered, and kept his own eyes on the man at his side.

But their luck seemed to be holding. Just ahead was the main hall-way, the wide entrance, the courtyard—and then the street! Uninterrupted, they reached the hallway, started across it and were just approaching the entrance—when another door at the other side of the reception hall opened, and out stepped Evan Carliotti with two of his men!

Carliotti's dark eyes stared, widened unbelievingly as he caught sight of the pseudo-guards and recognized them. His leonine face lost its color, his goatee quivered and his lips parted as if to shout a warning... but Operator 5 had already gone into action.

"Get them!" he snapped in that infinitesimal fraction of a second when Guy DeMott seemed on the point of flight.

Like a bullet, Jimmy launched himself across the hall, and his upswinging fist landed squarely on the point of the jaw of the husky bruiser beside the revolution chief. The guard had made a lightning draw from a shoulder holster, but now went down as if poleaxed. Then Jimmy was closing with Carliotti, ducking the man's flailing arms as he tore into the soft body and bent it double... as his strong fingers clutched at the thick throat and sought a grip on the windpipe.

Before Carliotti could more than half-gurgle the warning that was on his lips, he was down on his back. He threshed wildly on the floor, beating frantically at Jimmy's face in a desperate effort to break that grip. Savagely, as if strangling a foul monster whom he had interrupted in the midst of a red-handed murder, Jimmy put every ounce of his strength into his hold. Jaws clenched, lips curled up from his locked teeth, his arms trembled under the terrific pressure of his strong hands.

Out of the corner of his eye he caught flashes of DeMott struggling with the second of Carliotti's companions. They went down, clambered to their feet, backed across the hall toward the open entrance—and then saw DeMott tumbling down the steps with his antagonist on top of him.

But they did not matter. Carliotti was all that mattered—Carliotti, who was the fountainhead of all this horror and chaos; Carliotti, who would be emperor of all the world; Carliotti, who would grind America, and all it represented, under his heel. Inexorably that fearful grip tightened, dug deep into the bleeding flesh. Carliotti's eyes bulged horribly. His tongue stuck out of his gaping mouth, his face became so purple that it seemed the blood must burst from his cheeks… and then all of the resistance went out of him as he became a flabby thing that slumped back on the floor.

Evan Carliotti was dead!

Hardly believing what he had accomplished, Jimmy Christopher staggered to his feet, panting from his exertion. Now he saw that there were others running toward him—New Dawn troopers attracted by the mêlée. Horrified, they gaped at the body of their leader—and then their guns were out, blasting thunder in that domed hallway.

Past two of them Jimmy dived, while hot lead sought him close; and then he was clear. He was onto the steps, where a man sprawled grotesquely—and from somewhere Guy DeMott was yelling to him excitedly. Guy DeMott… there he was, leaping behind the wheel of a big car and flinging the rear door open for Jimmy.

"Carliotti's own bus!" he heard DeMott chuckle, as he flung himself into the rear compartment and pulled the door closed.

Evan Carliotti's limousine—what better 'open sesame' to speed them safely across the city the "Liberator" had turned into a wretched shambles?

## CHAPTER 9
## THE DEATHLESS ONE

**B**UT WHAT of that death-truck that had fled from the guillotine? Bullets had spattered against it as Bob Kent crouched low and sent the guillotine-tender hurtling on its way through the howling mob that milled in the Place de la Concorde. Glancing at the rear-view mirror, he had seen that President Tremel and Premier Montanye were lying flat on the floor. Trowbridge was trying to protect them with his own body. Perry and Boone were on their knees, blazing away at those who had broken through the gas barrage to get a foothold on the truck's side.

Then Perry was on his feet, teetering there crazily before he pitched over the side. Death had scored once, and a moment later it scored again as Nate Boone had followed his partner into the eager hands of the frustrated mob. Kent longed to stop the racing truck and empty his automatic into those snarling beasts—but grimly he held onto the wheel, eyes glued on the road ahead.

At last he was on the edge of the square, outdistancing the straggling pursuers—then tearing through a city that seemed deserted. All of Paris that could walk or crawl had jammed its way into the Place de la Concorde. And now the surrounding ruins were tenanted only by the human vultures who prowled through the sacked, fire-gutted buildings looking for loot missed by the earlier pillagers.

Past these looters the pitching, lurching truck raced across town to the Rue Montmartre, where the once gay sidewalk cafés were now dismal wrecks, bars overturned, tables and chairs heaps of ashes and twisted metal. Down the Montmartre Kent drove to a side street where a car was cached ready for a quick transfer—and then he was going back by another route, heading for the rendezvous in the Rue Danou.

A block from Number 66 he left the car and cautiously led the way on foot. Like the neighboring streets, the Rue Danou was silent and deserted. They encountered nobody as they turned in through the sagging arch of 66 and entered the court beyond. Larry Trowbridge, anxious to see his Clara, hurried on ahead.

He was across the main court, had almost reached the recessed entrance to the rear building, when it happened.

"Look out!" he yelled in sudden alarm. "A trap!"

He was racing back into the court, blazing away with the automatic Kent had given him. From the sides of the court, a hail of lead was now pouring.

At the first yell, Kent had hurled President Tremel behind him, catapulting him into Montanye with such force that both went down. This was all that saved their lives. Instantly Kent was on the stone flagging beside them, crawling backward crab-wise—dragging them with him as a storm of lead pelted against the arch.

Larry Trowbridge had almost reached it. He stopped to crouch for another shot, when his hand flew to his chest and he staggered back into the open like a sleepwalker… to be mowed down by a scything blast.

"No—no! Oh, God—no!" a woman's voice screamed shrilly, hysterically. "Larry—Larry!"

That was Clara Trowbridge, somewhere back there in the court. A prisoner, probably—held there as bait in case her husband and his companions had not walked into the waiting trap. Bob Kent thought quickly. It would be suicide to go back into that court, hopeless to try to rescue her. He was responsible for the safety of the president and the premier of France. Tight-lipped, he turned and led the way to where the escape car still awaited them.

Perry, Boone, and now Trowbridge—Death was reaping a heavy harvest that day. Perhaps by now Jimmy Christopher and the others had been added to the fatal list. Bob Kent, possibly, was the only survivor—but while he lived he had instructions to follow.

The first problem was to dispose of Tremel and Montanye before they were recognized and seized. A wrecked barroom halfway down the Rue Danou solved that problem. A popular American bar, it had been a gay resort until a few days ago, but now it was a rubbish-littered chaos, its contents looted, equipment wantonly destroyed—so completely ruined that not even the sorriest scavenger would give it a second glance.

Beneath the splintered and overturned bar, Kent found sufficient room for Tremel and Montanye to wedge their bodies. There, in the place that had once rung with American songs and laughter, the president and the premier of France cowered until the sun went down and darkness settled over the unlighted ruins that was Paris.

When Bob Kent returned for them he had found a safe but more comfortable hideout in a wrecked cottage in the now deserted suburb of Neuilly.

"Keep inside," he cautioned them. "Hide in the cellar if anyone approaches the building. Meanwhile I shall comb Paris in search of Operator 5. He may be dead, but I'll never be convinced of that until I see his body with my own eyes...."

But Bob Kent was nearly ready to give up hope, two days later, as he started to trudge wearily back to Neuilly. Nowhere had he found the least sign of Jimmy Christopher or the others. Nowhere had he been able to obtain the slightest inkling of their fate—when suddenly a hand clamped on his shoulder, whirling him around to face an old man in shabby workmen's clothing, with another who appeared to be his son.

"It's about time you decided to quit playing hide-and-seek," the straggly bearded oldster grunted—and Kent looked into the twinkling eyes of Jimmy Christopher and the skillfully transformed face of Guy DeMott.

"Thank God!" he breathed fervently. "I had almost given you up for lost." Quickly he told them of Larry Trowbridge's fate and then remembered Earl Seeley.

"Earl must have gone down in the Place de la Concorde," Jimmy Christopher softly phrased the obituary of another faithful member of his fast-dwindling band. "I lost track of him in the mêlée—but the next day we rescued his head from a pole near the guillotine.

"That means there are three of us left," he turned his thoughts resolutely to the present. "Three of us against a nation gone mad."

But those three were to perform miracles which are part of the history of France—miracles which were shrouded by secrecy and performed in the dead of night, while thousands of New Dawn agents sought them unceasingly....

FOR HOURS after they reached the Neuilly hideout, Jimmy consulted with Tremel and Montanye, and when at last that conference ended his plans were made. For a week he disappeared from Paris, and during that time an old man pedaled his way northward through the small towns and villages of France. An old man who stopped at little hovels for the night, who was hidden deep in wine cellars and even under piles of manure when inquisitive New Dawn agents came snooping.

Wherever he went his guarded questions took him to little back-room conferences where two or three anxious-eyed men welcomed him. And beside the name of each town in which he stopped he wrote at least one name on the little map he carried in his heavy shoe... the name of a citizen loyal to France and the sworn enemy of the New Dawn.

All the way to the Belgian border that trip continued, until at last he turned and retraced his way.

"The Maginot Line—that is your answer," he assured President Tremel when he rejoined that little company of hideaways in Neuilly. "France built that great line of fortifications as a bulwark for her freedom—and that is what we will make it. When the troops went over to the New Dawn, they swarmed out of those underground quarters they detested so much. They destroyed what they could, but the storerooms deep in the earth are still filled with food and ammunition."

He pointed out, "Just north of Sedan is a point that is scarcely damaged. You can take it over and hold it with a few hundred men, if you are discovered. There should be nearly that number there now—and there will be more to greet you when you arrive."

Nearly five hundred loyal Frenchmen were gathered at the concentration point when President Tremel and Premier

Montanye ran the dangerous gauntlet of the "underground railway" Jimmy Christopher had established, and daily the number increased as new arrivals came by ones and twos.

"It is a tremendous task that faces us," the gaunt-cheeked president told them. "We must build a new France—cradle and nurse it here until we are strong enough to step out and come to grips with the vandals who have overrun our land. This tremendous task we are permitted to undertake only because of the efforts and sacrifices of Operator 5 and his companions. It is a debt which the new France must never forget!"

It is history how Pierre Tremel met that critical situation; how he transformed the office of the French presidency from the innocuous role of corner-stone-layer it had become to that of inspired leader and nation-builder; how he reshaped the destiny of France from the underground burrows where he and his faithful followers hid away from the New Dawn spies.

Operator 5 served with him tirelessly, and, as he watched the new organization taking form—as he watched the new France coming to life—he knew that the days of anarchy and chaos were numbered.

There was a long, arduous trail ahead... but at the end of it there would be a rebirth for the prostrate and ruined French nation....

But as he watched Tremel and his associates labor for their country, Jimmy's thoughts turned more and more anxiously to America. Vainly he had been trying in every way to get in touch with the United States—but that proved impossible. Trans-Atlantic communications were entirely in the hands of the New

Dawn regime. So completely had they throttled every means of communication with the outer world that even the radios had been confiscated—destroyed by the New Dawn commissioners in charge of each village and hamlet.

In less than a month, France had been shorn of Twentieth Century every-day conveniences and thrust back into the Middle Ages. However, no official decrees could destroy the inventive genius of the French mechanics—and Jimmy Christopher. Patiently they worked, gathering bits of discarded radios here and there, fashioning new elements, and then repairing the sabotaged ruin that had been made of the electric plant which supplied power to that section of the Maginot Line.

Days of patient labor… but at last their efforts were rewarded. The reconstructed set worked. But when Jimmy Christopher tuned in America he almost wished that he had remained in ignorance of the news that came whispering through the air!

"The Great Lakes states are now almost completely under the domination of the fast-spreading New Dawn regime," a news broadcaster announced.

The New Dawn had broken out in America! Incredulously Jimmy listened as those portentous words came through the loud-speaker.

"With Chicago and Pittsburgh as its strongholds, the insurrection has spread deep into Kentucky and threatens to sweep eastward through Pennsylvania and New York. General Horatio Morgan, on the east, and Major-General Arthur Chadwick, in the south, are marshaling every man to stem the advance. But their defense is handicapped by disaffection, which breaks out persistently at their rear, and by the morale-shattering effect of the New Dawn troopers, the deathless men who sweep everything before them!"

The deathless men? Jimmy groped in vain for an explanation of that amazing phrase which fell so matter-of-fact from the announcer's lips. Vainly he tried to figure out its meaning—but there was none. Evidently everyone in America was completely familiar with the term. And evidently these "deathless men" were responsible for the New Dawn's success.

For success it was—there could be no doubt about that. As Jimmy listened, his heart sank with the realization that Andrew Warren was putting up a desperate, losing fight—frantically trying to stem a tide of revolution that threatened to engulf the entire nation. There was no word of government victories, or government offensives. Everywhere the New Dawn seemed to be gaining while the harassed government commanders strove to hold them back.

America torn by revolution, faced with the anarchy that had engulfed France—and he thousands of miles away!

"We're going back!" Operator 5 snapped as the broadcast concluded. But as he looked into the tense faces of Bob Kent and Guy DeMott, the same question was mirrored in their eyes. How?

There was no chance to board a liner in France or in Belgium, which had also fallen under the domination of the New Dawn. The only way was to reach England, and there secure passage to America. But between them and England lay more than a hundred and fifty miles of France, and then the width of the English Channel....

"I have relatives in a fishing village a few miles from Boulogne," Guy DeMott offered thoughtfully as they sat trying to plan a way to span that distance. "Or at least I did have until this business started. If we could reach there, they should be able to locate a boat for us."

**THE TRIP** to Boulogne was beset with perils, but gray-bearded old "Papa Bove" and his two sons finally made it. They arrived at the little hamlet of Chaunay, where fishing was the business of life. Here the New Dawn meant very little to the simple-minded folk who accepted with a shrug the commissioner and his assistants who came to direct their destinies. DeMott, who had gone on ahead from Boulogne, had located his relatives, and when Jimmy and Bob Kent arrived a hiding-place was ready for them.

Jules Monet, a distant cousin of Guy's, was one of Chaunay's most substantial citizens. He ran a fleet of fishing boats and maintained a lodging house for his crews, where the newcomers could not only sleep but prepare their own meals as well.

"The boats are out now and the house is empty," Guy greeted the new arrivals. "We can put up there, and nobody will be the wiser. Old Jules will help us with the boat, too. It may take several days, but he knows where he can buy a motor-dinghy large enough to get us across in calm weather. He is negotiating for it now—casually, so as not to arouse the suspicions of the commissioner the New Dawn put in here to boss the place."

The "several days" became nearly a week—and with each passing evening Jimmy's uneasiness increased. Since Guy DeMott had rescued him from the Luxembourg Palace he had striven hard to convince himself that his suspicions of the man were unfounded. He had succeeded—almost. But now the old doubts were recurring. DeMott was acting strangely—was away entirely too frequently in conducting the mysterious negotiations for this boat.

Besides, Jimmy had detected a vague air of guilt about the man—a hesitancy and evasiveness that was unmistakable. Guy DeMott tried hard to conceal it, but gave every evidence of a man engaged in something underhanded and scheming to betray his comrades....

Then the day of the boat's delivery arrived.

"It will be here about twelve-thirty," DeMott told them early that morning when he came back from a visit to Monet's house. "It will be tied up at the end of old Jules' wharf, under the shed, and he will have the wharf cleared for us by one o'clock. Till then, he wants us to keep out of sight."

This sounded fine, but when Jimmy glanced at Bob Kent he saw his own suspicion mirrored in Bob's eyes. DeMott was excited, naturally, but there was something more to it than that. He was concealing something from them.

"I'm going to keep a watch on that wharf this morning," Kent said quietly, as soon as he had an opportunity to speak to Jimmy alone. Shortly after that he went to his room.

DeMott, likewise, had disappeared. Uneasily Jimmy paced the floor and walked repeatedly to the small-paned window to look out over the quiet harbor. But that window was of little use. Its view of half of the harbor was obstructed, and that half included Monet's wharf.

Nine, nine-thirty, almost ten.... The minutes seemed to drag by, and Jimmy could not master his agitation. Somehow, he felt that there was something afoot. A persistent warning rang in his subconscious mind....

Abruptly he decided to find Guy DeMott, face him frankly with his suspicions. But just as he reached the head of the stairs, a door at the other end of the corridor opened—DeMott's door. Out stepped a figure that was a dead ringer of Jimmy himself—a counterpart of his gray-bearded 'Papa Bove' disguise!

Noiselessly Jimmy eased himself down the stairs and drew back into the shadow of a doorway on the ground-floor level. Guy DeMott was coming down softly, furtively. DeMott's eyes glanced warily at Jimmy's door, then at the kitchen where Jimmy or Bob Kent might be. He was heading for the back door, which he could reach without passing through any of the rooms.

DeMott was slipping out of the house, disguised as Jimmy, heading for the boat, which must be there at the wharf now—at ten o'clock, *instead of at one as he had notified them!*

But before DeMott could reach that back door, Jimmy stepped out and barred his way!

FOR AN instant DeMott seemed taken aback, to cringe— then like a tiger he leaped forward. His fingers sought Jimmy's throat, as he rushed him back against the wall, fighting with silent desperation.

Carefully Jimmy avoided those clutching fingers. His hands slipped around DeMott to secure the grip that would paralyze him. But before they were in place—before he could exert the numbing pressure—something crashed down on his head with stunning force. The barrel of an automatic that had suddenly appeared in DeMott's hand.

"No, you don't!" he heard DeMott grit.

Then the room was swaying dizzily, sickeningly, the walls bellying and falling in on Jimmy as he slumped to the floor. He could see DeMott bending over him, carefully arranging his slightly disordered make-up. DeMott opened the door, glancing warily up and down before he slipped out. Then a blast of shots greeted his appearance! Shots rained against the side of the house spitting through the panels of the door as it flung half-open—DeMott's head and shoulders crashing against it....

That ambuscade snapped Jimmy out of his coma. Crawling to his knees, he reached the door, stared down at DeMott's sprawled form, lying over the threshold. Guy DeMott was already covered with blood that poured from half a dozen wounds. He lay like one dead. Yet his glassy eyes were still open, staring up through the doorway. They caught a glimpse of Jimmy's face, and the stiffening lips moved.

"No... no," he whispered. "Don't come any closer... that may ruin everything. Stay there, Jimmy... for God's sake! I think they've gone... but wait and be sure. I knew they were waiting out here... that's why I put on this rig and came out. It was the only way. They've been on your trail... wouldn't have quit until they had gotten you... sooner or later. Now they think you are dead... and you will be safe...."

"You knew they were waiting?"

"I knew all along that you suspected me, Operator 5," came in a mere whisper. "So I used that… played it up and made you think I was going to betray you… so that you would watch me and not have an opportunity to step into their trap. I knew you would see me upstairs there… knew you would stop me. It was the only way… to keep you in here long enough… to trick Evan Carliotti's killers."

"Carliotti's?" Jimmy wondered.

"He isn't dead," DeMott gasped. "I saw him here in Chaunay… last night… looking for you. Saw him…." The last word was only a wisp of sound that came from dead lips, and, as it passed, a great stillness settled over the house—the stillness of eternity, it seemed. Jimmy Christopher stared down at the dead, disguised features and realized how completely he had been tricked—tricked into saving his own life by the man he had suspected of being a Judas….

## CHAPTER 10
## ZERO HOUR

HOW LONG Jimmy crouched there just inside the doorway he never knew. Then suddenly he realized that men were coming toward the house. They emerged cautiously from the cover to which they had run when that murderous volley roared. In a moment they would be here in the doorway, gaping open-mouthed at two Papa Boves, asking a lot of questions.

Jimmy did not wait for that. Running back down the little

corridor, he reached the kitchen, crossed it, and opened a window on the other side of the house. Stepping out quickly, he darted to cover and skirted the building beyond, to steer a course straight for Monet's wharf.

The little pier was deserted, as he walked to the low boat-shed at its end. There was the motor-dinghy for which they had been waiting, a figure stretched flat on the planks beside it. Bob Kent, with his throat awesomely cut from ear to ear!

The dinghy had arrived at ten instead of one, but Death had come with it as a passenger. Death that would have claimed all three of them had it not been for Guy DeMott's heroic sacrifice.

Jimmy Christopher stepped down into the little cockleshell and untied the ropes that held it, tugging at the motor string until it chugged into life. Then he nosed his way out of the shed, the prow headed for England. As he crouched low in the little craft, he looked back at the village he was leaving. The wharf was still deserted. Apparently nobody had seen him go—unless perhaps that woman who stood on the fish pier next to Monet's, shading her eyes as she looked out over the Channel.

For just an instant she was there, and then she had vanished. Jimmy dismissed her from his mind as he stared out over the expanse of water that lay between him and the safety in Great Britain.

Evan Carliotti was still alive…. That amazing fact was almost unbelievable. The man had been dead beyond any question when he dropped from Jimmy's hands on the floor of the Luxembourg Palace entrance. And yet Guy DeMott had seen him not once

At that moment, every door of the courtroom burst open with deliverers!

125

but several times there in Chaunay, directing the killers who must have been following Jimmy's trail all these days....

The thing was inexplicable. But the deadly effectiveness of Carliotti's spy system was all too well established. Of the eight men who had come to Europe with Jimmy, not one now remained alive. One by one, Carliotti's agents had cut them down, until Operator 5 was the lone survivor—one man to fight against a world now wildly aflame in both hemispheres!

The dinghy cleaved a path through the choppy currents. For nearly three hours he sat there, guiding his course only by a compass, vainly wishing for wings to speed him over those thousands of watery miles to America. But at last the white cliffs of England rose palely before him, became more distinct as he drew closer and picked out the dark smudge that was the harbor of Folkestone.

At least the first leg of the journey was completed. Jimmy heaved a sigh of relief as he approached the channel-boat dock and saw the flag waving over its buildings. The Union Jack! But the multi-crossed banner seemed darker than usual—oddly unfamiliar. Jimmy strained his eyes, and a cold chill ran down his spine as the wind straightened the bunting in the sun. Instead of the familiar colors, he saw that the background of this flag was black—ebon black with a splash of orange in its center and rising to its top.

The flag of the New Dawn!

Instantly, Jimmy's hand reached out and grabbed the tiller, pulled it toward him and swerved the dinghy in a crescent that would take him clear of that ominous banner. With the New Dawn in control, Folkestone certainly offered him no haven.

But he was too late. Already sharp eyes on the shore had noticed his arrival, seen that shift of course—and now several fast-traveling boats were setting out to overhaul him. Helplessly, he sat there as the little dinghy motor put-putted ineffectually—it was no match whatever for those swift cruisers. Speedily they crept up on him, and then fired a warning shot dangerously close.

Jimmy ignored it, holding his automatic ready. Twice it barked defiance—and then the dinghy was overhauled, ridden down and smashed to pieces as one of the pursuers crashed into it. Stunned and dripping wet, they fished him out of the water. They ripped the false whiskers from his face as half a dozen men grinned at his discomfiture.

"Papa Bove—alias Operator 5!" their leader jeered. "Evan Carliotti will be very pleased to meet you again. Perhaps this time he will offer you the same comfortable cell you arranged for him the last time you were in England! Things have changed a bit since those days, Operator 5. Now is our day—the day of the New Dawn!"

AS HE listened to this boasting, Jimmy's worst fears were realized. Despite the warnings he had given Sir John Fraser, despite the raids the British Secret Service had staged, the New Dawn malcontents had triumphed. They had seized Birmingham, London and the whole lower portion of England and were getting ready to push their conquest beyond the Scottish border.

The king and queen had fled to Scotland, and all opposition

to the New Dawn seemed to have been stifled. Evan Carliotti was in the saddle, grinding his foes underfoot.

*Evan Carliotti*—that was the most stupefying part of it! Evan Carliotti had been in Chaunay directing his killers that very morning, and yet these fellows boasted that he was in London, established in Buckingham Palace, from which he had routed the royal family!

Triumphantly his captors bore Jimmy to London and took him before the central revolutionary committee. Once more he came face to face with Evan Carliotti. The leonine head towered above him and nodded with approval, the gray goatee quivered as Carliotti chuckled with satisfaction.

Jimmy stared at that face searchingly… and then the mystery began to unravel. This was *not* the Carliotti with whom he had fought in the Luxembourg Palace! This man was heavier, more gross—but not sufficiently so to be noticeable except under the strictest scrutiny. This man was a double of Evan Carliotti's!

That explained many things—how Carliotti could be in America, on a ship at sea, in England and in France all at the same time. The wily rabble-rouser was taking no chances with his own skin. Before he had entered upon the precarious pastime of world-conquering, he had taken out insurance on his life by providing himself with a dozen cleverly counterparted and well trained doubles who did all the dangerous contact work in his guise while *he* sat back at a safe distance and directed them all!

Undoubtedly, at that moment, the real Evan Carliotti was safe somewhere in France, well guarded by his New Dawn troopers.

Jimmy could not but respect the fellow's genius—and with

that acknowledgment came a fresh realization of the supreme danger to America this man represented. Evan Carliotti was no careless blunderer, no stupid egotist who would destroy himself. He was an evil genius who would be a constant threat and menace to the free institutions of the world as long as he lived....

"Excellent—excellent!" the pseudo-Carliotti applauded his men. "It is always a pleasure to entertain Operator 5, and this time I trust we may be able to keep you with us more successfully than on the past occasions. This time I think your stay with us will be very, very long."

His dark eyes were gloating. But as Jimmy returned their stare, he glimpsed something more in their depths, read a barely restrained curiosity—speculation that would not quiet down. These duplicate Carliottis must, of course, be kept closely posted on one another's activities. But they were still human, still curious. In that might lie the one weakness, the Achilles' heel, in Evan Carliotti's clever scheming.

Jimmy had to gamble on it.

"It looks as if you hold all the cards, Carliotti," he admitted glumly as the guards started to lead him away. "A man can't hold out against the whole world." But as he passed close to the smugly smiling leader his voice dropped, his words came in little more than a whisper. "I think now I will listen to that proposition you made me in America."

Then he was out of the room, being escorted to a cell in the grim old Tower of London that was the New Dawn headquarters.

129

WOULD THE trick work? Jimmy wondered. He had caught just a flash of the pseudo-Carliotti's face as he passed, seen the flicker of interest. The fellow would be thinking now. If Jimmy's gamble worked, he would nibble at the bait, try to learn the nature of that "proposition" his American counterpart had made.

If that gamble worked, Jimmy must be prepared. As soon as he was alone in his cell he took off his three-strand leather belt and unhooked the buckle. Unwinding the loose binding which held the strands together, they opened into one continuous length—a leather rope nine feet long. Carefully Jimmy fastened one end of it near the top of a cell bar. Then he waited... until after dark.

It was nearly eight o'clock when Carliotti came down the corridor, to pause outside the cell door and look in at the prisoner.

Jimmy's pulses pounded. There was no mistaking the cupidity in the fellow's glance.

"Tomorrow you will come before the revolutionary court, and I suppose you realize what their verdict will be," Carliotti announced. "Then it will be too late for me to do anything for you. But tonight, if there is anything you want to tell me, any offer you want to make...."

Jimmy noticed that the fellow's voice was low, guarded. When he spoke, his own tone was little more than a whisper. "You wanted me to deliver President Warren into your hands," he husked. "You suggested that together you and I could...."

Now his words were so low that Carliotti could not hear. The man came closer, stood just outside the cell door. Then the leather rope, which Jimmy Christopher had been clutching, as he stood with one hand gripping the top of a cell bar, suddenly sailed out and came down over Carliotti's head. In a flash Jimmy had it pulled tight, closing the noose around the fellow's neck!

Carliotti gasped, clutched frantically at the leather strand—but it had already bitten too deeply into his flesh. His tongue gagged out of his mouth and gurgling noises came from his constricting throat.

"The keys!" Jimmy rasped in his ear. "Open this cell door if you want to live, Carliotti!"

The strangling man gasped something that was unintelligible. One hand floundered toward his pocket. But at that instant a dark figure hurtled across the corridor and grasped the leather rope. A knife flashed and snipped the thong in two. Pawing at his throat, Carliotti staggered back from the door—and then turned fearful, cowering eyes to the stern-faced individual who confronted him.

"Fool!" the rescuer rasped. "You haven't sufficient brains to be treacherous. But this will make a fine report!"

Grasping Carliotti by the arm, he started him down the corridor as if a truant being taken back to school. Jimmy's high hopes plummeted, as their voices faded. He had been within a few seconds of success, but Evan Carliotti seemed to have overlooked nothing. Even these doubles who carried out his orders were shadowed so that they could not betray him. Against a man so perfectly entrenched it seemed useless to struggle....

OPERATOR 5'S spirits were low that night, but they touched bottom next morning when he was taken before the revolutionary court—and again faced a Carliotti in the role of chief magistrate. Again he heard himself condemned and sentenced to death, but this Carliotti took spiteful delight in passing sentence.

"You seem to have a penchant for escaping from cells, Operator 5," he sneered. "Now I shall not bother to return you to one. Your sentence will be carried out immediately. Bailiff, you will deliver the prisoner to the executioner."

Jimmy Christopher looked all around that crowded courtroom. Seven judges were up there on the bench, nearly fifty New Dawn officials and hangers-on in the spectators chairs below them. A score of yellow-shirted troopers were posted around the chamber. There was not a friendly face in the lot—not so much as a ray of hope among them.

Now the bailiff, flanked by half a dozen guards, was coming forward. This was the end—the zero hour. Nothing remained now, except the last desperate expedient which Operator 5 always held in reserve. His eyes still holding Carliotti's triumphant leer, the fingers of his right hand fastened around the curiously shaped ring on the third finger of his left, started to turn the top of it.

Contained in the hollow top of that ring was a quantity of the most powerful explosive known to man. It was sufficient to blow himself into eternity and wipe out with him all of this New Dawn regime. With this nest of plotters blown to atoms, England might be able to throw off the New Dawn yoke and show America the way back to freedom.

Jimmy's jaws clenched. The top of his ring started to open—

and at that moment every door of that courtroom was suddenly thrown wide open. Framed in each doorway was a phalanx of grim-faced men armed with rifles and revolvers. Those weapons poured a deadly hail into the New Dawners.

That first blasting volley created wild havoc. Too startled to yell, men died before they knew what had happened. They died as they tried frantically to leap from their seats and find a way to safety—died as they pitched from the bench. Carliotti alone of those judges managed to get to his feet, but before he could turn and flee he screamed horribly... a scream that choked into silence as he toppled on his face.

The New Dawn troopers made an attempt to return that fire, but were cut down where they stood. The bailiff and his men were caught in mid-stride and hurled back—into death.

That much Jimmy saw as he flung himself flat on the floor and crawled to a place of comparative safety. Like rats in a trap those New Dawn zealots were dying, and now the triumphant attackers swarmed into the room—grim-faced purposeful Englishmen, with Sir John Fortescue at their head. Yet they were not all Englishmen.

Jimmy blinked in unbelieving amazement. That small, wiry little devil who came running toward him, his pug-nosed face wrinkled into a delighted grin—was Tim Donovan! Tim was followed by five mere youngsters—lads no older than himself and all of them Americans!

"A clean sweep, Jimmy!" Tim shouted, as he came racing up and threw his arm around Operator 5's shoulders. "We nabbed them all—the whole New Dawn executive committee! We were planning to close in on them later in the week, but when we heard about you we had to advance the program a bit. This will be the end of the New Dawn in London!"

Gradually Jimmy calmed him to coherence and learned how Tim and his own volunteers had come to England to search for him—how they had contacted Sir John Fortescue and had been working with the British Secret Service to undermine and overthrow the New Dawn.

And then Sir John was there at Jimmy's side, shaking his hand and smiling.

"You have this young fellow to thank for your life, Operator 5." He nodded to where Tim shuffled uneasily. "And I think Great Britain has him to thank for the end of the New Dawn. This was his *coup* this morning—and it has just about wiped out the revolutionists' organization in London. Now it will be an easy matter to close in on them and mop them up in the surrounding cities."

Operator 5 listened, and beads of perspiration oozed out on his forehead even though the day was not warm. Death had swooped so close that he had fairly felt the chill touch of the black wings. Slowly, carefully, with fingers that trembled ever so slightly, he twisted the skeleton-head top of his death-ring back into place....

## CHAPTER 11
## CRIMSON DAWN

**M**ERCIFUL SEMI-CONSCIOUSNESS had enveloped Diane Elliot as her captors dragged her down from the roof and back into the house where she had been quarantined. Vaguely she was aware that they were carrying her out of the building, trundling her through the darkness, and then into another building that was chill and damp. Then she was dropped onto something hard and uncomfortable. A clanging filled her ears—and then came silence....

As soon as she awoke and glanced around her, Diane knew she was in jail—she was in a cell that was barely illuminated by a thin beam of light from the late-rising moon. And then came a flood of memory....

Something had gone terribly wrong. Somehow Henry Pfeiffer's plan had miscarried. The men who had closed in on her had not hesitated to grab her. They had shown no fear of contagion, and yet Pfeiffer had proclaimed that she was suffering from a virulent fever which might mean death for any who contracted it. They must have disbelieved him, and perhaps he had already paid with his life for his deception....

Diane had plenty of time to wonder about Pfeiffer's fate, in the days that followed. Long days when she sat alone in her cell or paced back and forth to the window from which she could look out onto one of the main streets.

Three times a day a guard brought her food, and gradually she managed to win his good will. But when she tried to ask questions about "the doctor" he became close-mouthed. Pfeiffer's fate, it seemed, had been settled and was not to be discussed.

Tim was another constant worry on Diane's mind. Had he received her magnesium-flare warning? Had he sped back to Washington with the news of her capture—or impulsively attempted to come to her aid, himself, and also fallen into a trap? That must be the answer, she told herself, as the days went by without any sign of a rescue.

Daily she gazed out onto the street, keen eyes searching for a possible rescuer—but none came. She scanned the sky hopefully, but always it was empty... until the morning when there came the roar of an airplane motor overhead. Eagerly she dashed to the window, and quickly identified the approaching speck as an Army machine!

Overhead it circled, and then seemed to swoop down for a landing. Was the pilot attempting to reach her? He would be captured surely! If only he had reconnoitered and then gone back for help! Tensely she waited, expecting at any moment to hear the crackle of shots. Long minutes went past, nearly half an hour. Then again the air was filled with the roar of the engine as the plane ascended and slowly faded in the east—on its way back to Washington!

Frantically, Diane endeavored to answer the questions that filled her mind. How was it the Army flyer had been allowed to land here in Honesdale—and then depart again? Had they tricked him so that he would go back and report that there was nothing wrong here?

All hope for help was gone. As Diane sat on her cot, she realized that if she was to escape it must be by her own efforts. The jail, she noticed, had suffered with the rest of Honesdale when the Purple raiders had battered their way through the town. However, one wing of it was still intact. That small wing gave her barely sufficient space to exercise, when her guard let her have the run of the place. It, too, had been shaken by the explosion that had wrecked the rest of the building. Its walls were cracked and looked none too secure… and in that she found a ray of hope.

With tools made from a fork and spoon she had managed to slip from her tray, when her guard was not over-observant, she set to work on one of those cracks. Digging and boring, she widened it little by little. Slow, painful work, it would take weeks before she could hope for success. All that time the New Dawn might be perpetrating its deviltry. But at least she was doing something, could hold out *some* hope.

She needed that ray of hope in the days that followed, for now her worst fears were realized. The New Dawn had come out from hiding, and flared into open rebellion!

"It was nasty going for a while, but we cleaned up just the way we knew we would," she heard a visitor in the little jail office telling her guard. "Pittsburgh is ours, and the cities all around are joining us one after the other. Give us another week, Jake, and we'll have Chicago and every town between here and there. This time the New Dawn has come to stay. Too bad Operator 5 can't be here to enjoy it!"

It explained the unusual activity Diane had noticed in the streets during the past few days. Trucks had been coming and going from the mills in a regular procession, delivering war material to the New Dawn mob—arming them with a weapon that would rout their dismayed opponents. That weapon she could expose, if only she could reach Washington....

With renewed energy, she went back to her tedious labor, until her fingers were raw and bleeding—but the progress she had made was almost nothing! Weak, discouraged, Diane was on the verge of tears that night as she slumped dejectedly on her cot. It would take not weeks but months, perhaps even years, to escape in this way. Now hours, even minutes, were infinitely precious. Somehow she *must* get out of there....

And then it seemed that her prayer was miraculously answered!

SUDDENLY THE night was filled with a terrific explosion that seemed to rend the very earth. The floor shook and trembled under her feet; the building groaned, and she could hear stones crashing and tumbling—could hear screams and yells outside as other buildings capsized. Tense, hardly daring to move, Diane crouched there and listened to the rumbling roar that filled her cell, seemed to engulf her.

Dust was in her nostrils, choking her, stones rolling across the floor. Now she saw what had happened. The side wall—the very wall she had been weakening with her constant gnawing—had *collapsed!* The tumbled rubble half-filled the cell. When she climbed up onto it, she could look out through a hole that was larger than her body, could climb out into the night. She was free!

Carefully picking her way through the debris, Diane stepped

out onto the street and darted through the darkness. Honesdale, she now saw, had grown since she was imprisoned. There were far more people in the town, and new houses had been slapped up to accommodate them. Workers in the mills and factories—busily turning out arms and ammunition for the New Dawn.

It was an explosion in one of those ammunition plants that had liberated her. It had also filled the town with dead and maimed victims. Dozens of them were being carried through the streets to impromptu hospitals, and Honesdale had become a stricken town filled with white-faced men and screaming, wailing women.

She ran little chance of being recognized in that turmoil, Diane realized as she worked her way through the shadows. Honesdale had other things to think of that night....

Suddenly she drew back and plastered herself against the brick wall of a building while she stared unbelievingly. The man who had just passed—was *Henry Pfeiffer!* Henry Pfeiffer, grim-jawed and narrow-eyed, striding tensely down the street. He was paying no attention to the wounded all around him, and yet he had been posing here in Honesdale as a doctor. That curious thought filled her mind even before she realized that he should not even have been there at all. He should now be dead, because their scheme had been discovered!

Subconsciously her feet moved forward. Almost without her own volition she followed him at a safe distance; to a building at which he turned in. This was no hospital. It looked more like a meeting place, as if it might have been the old Honesdale town hall. The double doors were wide open, and she dared to follow him. Down the main hall he strode and into a lighted room at the rear of the building. Excited voices issued from it.

Diane followed, found a small anteroom next to the lighted one. Crouching there in the darkness, she listened—amazed at what she heard.

"We can't let this stop us," a man's voice was declaring grimly. "It's tragic, of course, but there are thousands of men depending on us to keep them supplied. We've got to work doubly hard. Somehow we will have to make up for the loss of Fernald's factory. I don't care how, *we've got to do it,* you understand!"

That was Henry Pfeiffer talking. Henry Pfeiffer giving orders, laying down the law and exhorting them to increased activity for the New Dawn. Henry Pfeiffer, who seemed to be the leader of this outfit instead of the prisoner she had supposed him.

What manner of man was this? A traitor? Had he sold out America to these New Dawners in order to save his own life? Or was he tricking them? Had he taken them in so completely that they believed he was leading them on to success? But such a thing was incredible. It would have taken all the art of a super-confidence man to twist them around his finger that way—after the fiasco of her escape from his quarantine....

DIANE COULD not attempt to understand Pfeiffer, as she slipped warily out of that building, but she knew that she wanted Washington to know of the man's activities. Somehow, she must reach the capital and reveal what she had learned. There seemed but one way for her to leave Honesdale, and that was on foot. Unchallenged, she reached the outskirts of the stricken city and trudged out onto the dark road that led to Pittsburgh, the capital of the New Dawn.

It was nearly dawn when she reached the Smoky City and managed to find a room in a shabby lodging-house. Already she had seen the scars of the New Dawn rebellion—factories and mills in ruins, looted stores, and fire-gutted buildings that had once been offices and homes of Pittsburgh's loyal citizens. When she ventured forth that afternoon, she saw sights that sickened her.

Pittsburgh was a stricken city that had been turned over to the mob. Pillaging gangs marauded in every direction; outrage followed outrage. This was a sample of what would happen to all America when the poisonous cancer had spread from the Atlantic to the Pacific.

And it *was* spreading—on every hand she heard reports of New Dawn victories. Posted in the public squares were huge maps with the yellow blot, that was New Dawn conquered territory, spreading out and creeping over state after state. It would be only a question of time before that destroying tide reached New York and Washington—and drown the last effort at resistance.

Nothing seemed to be able to stem the yellow tide; nobody seemed to be able to arrest its gathering momentum. Nobody....

But surely Operator 5 would not be idle at a time like this. Surely he must be doing something. But what? Where was Jimmy Christopher? Diane vainly asked herself that question a thousand times, little knowing that the man for whom she prayed was thousands of miles away....

FRANCE WAS in the hands of the New Dawn. But up along the northern border, in the sanctuary of the Maginot Line, was an organization that, Jimmy Christopher was convinced, would eventually work out the nation's salvation. London had overthrown the New Dawn, and the battle against the revolutionists was being triumphantly carried from town to town. In a few weeks the New Dawn would be a thing of the past on British soil.

That left only America, but the news that came across the ocean grew steadily worse. City after city was falling to the rebellion, and Jimmy fretted and fumed as the slow-moving hours dragged past. It seemed that he and Tim and young Donovan's companions would never be on their way... but at last the *Imperator* steamed out of Southampton and headed into the west.

Joe Carey, Nick Faroni, Peter Tully, Ken Rockwell and Harry Walton—those five youngsters were a crew picked as carefully as any Operator 5 ever had recruited. Five young Americans taken from the city streets—from the gutters, perhaps. But Tim Donovan knew his men, and that any one of that little crew would unhesitating have laid down his life for the others or the cause they served.

Operator 5 studied them with surreptitious admiration, as they crowded around him in the wireless operator's cabin and listened to the short-wave broadcast coming in from America. Eager young faces were tense and taut, flashing eyes darkened ominously, nervous hands balled into fists, as they longed to come to grips with those vandals who were seizing the land of liberty and turning it into a mob-ridden hell.

"General Morgan's troops are putting up desperate resistance every foot of the way," came the voice of the announcer, "but they seem unable to check the New Dawn advance. With the fall of Harrisburg and Wilkes-Barre, the fate of Philadelphia seems determined. Within a week, the New Dawn commanders predict, their shock troops will lead the way into New York and Washington and the subjugation of America will be complete."

It was those shock troops that baffled Jimmy. How an undisciplined mob could stand up against the best troops the government sent against them and defeat them in every clash, was something he could not understand. On the battlefield the New Dawners seemed to be supreme soldiers—but in the territory they conquered they seemed to be a lawless mob.

"News that penetrates through the New Dawn lines continues to astound and horrify the nation," the commentator was saying. "Pittsburgh, Chicago, Columbus, and most of the New Dawn centers are helpless in the grip of mob rule. Fires are blazing unchecked, and private property has been seized. This whole section of America has been sacked, and now the pillagers are hungrily pressing on to more spoils...."

"And those are Americans!" Tim Donovan marveled as the dire news flowed from the loud speaker. "It sounds impossible. I can't understand how our people can sink to such a level. Unless—" he thought aloud—"this is the effect of the drugs their leaders are feeding them."

Drugs was the answer! Drug-inflamed mobs, little better than bands of beasts in human form—that was Evan Carliotti's answer to the problem of subjugating a free America. The "liberation" he offered these poor dupes was a drug-inspired debauch that would leave them hopelessly enslaved when the rioting was over....

Operator 5 listened to those maddening reports, as day by day the coast of America drew closer. One day more now—then they would be in New York!

BUT THAT evening, as he approached the wireless cabin, Jimmy caught the sounds of a struggle. Quickly he led the way, yanked open the cabin door—to find the bloody-faced operator desperately fighting with four huskies of the crew, while another was busy reducing the receiving set to a tangle of battered junk.

Jimmy Christopher dived through the doorway and into the very center of that cowardly pack.

"Look out!" one of them yelled a wild alarm, but it was too late.

Jimmy's gun barrel crashed down over the fellow's head, knocked him insensible. Then he was darting to one side, ducking the blow of a heavy belaying-pin as he battered his gun into the teeth of another of the panic-stricken attackers. Frantically, they tried to flee. But Tim Donovan and his companions were there in the doorway, leaping into the fray with eager delight. Too long had they been forced to sit there helplessly listening to the radio reports of New Dawn outrages. Now, at last, they could come to grips with flesh-and-blood adversaries to combat.

The battle was all too short to suit them. Hardly begun, it was finished when the wireless man's assailants lay beaten into insensibility or cowering on the floor, howling for mercy.

"What is it all about, Dick?" Jimmy urged, as he knelt beside the battered Sparks, wiping the blood from his face. "Why did they jump you?"

The operator was on the verge of collapse, but his eyes opened and his lips quivered.

"The New Dawn," he managed to gasp. "Their army has taken New York, and they are seizing control of the ship. They didn't want you to know—wanted us to take the ship right into their hands...."

His voice faded and he lapsed into unconsciousness. But Jimmy had already heard sufficient—New York had fallen to the New Dawn! With lightning speed, his brain was clicking, planning, meeting this calamitous development now suddenly confronting him.

"We can't let them get away with it!" he snapped. "We've got to get control of this ship, take it to a port farther south— to Baltimore. Tim, you take Carey and Rockwell and Walton. Get to the head of the engine-room. Two of you take the port-side door, two the starboard. Get inside those doors and close them behind you. From the upper landing you can get the drop on the whole engine-room. Get it and keep it. See that every man stays there on his job, even if you have to shoot down half a dozen to make them understand.... You, Tully and Faroni— come with me. We're going to the bridge to see that the course is properly changed."

A mob of sailors tried to stop them halfway to the bridge. But a volley of well aimed shots quickly set them back on their heels—and, when Jimmy and his companions charged them, they broke in panic. Jimmy led the way to the bridge, where

Captain Bankhead cowered beneath the threatening gun muzzle of a mutineer.

Jimmy Christopher and the assailant saw each other at the same moment, and it seemed that simultaneously their guns roared. But the split-second, that means the difference between life and death, was in Jimmy's favor. The mutineer dropped without a sound, a bullet through his heart.

Jimmy turned to confront the trembling captain. "We're changing out course, Captain—going down to Baltimore," he commanded, and saw how the officer's face blanched.

"We can't—we can't do that!" Captain Bankhead quavered. "They are too many for us. They will break in here and kill us all. They have control of the ship. It's no use trying to oppose them—the New Dawn is winning everywhere. They will have the whole country within a week, and we'll be marked men if we try to oppose them now."

"We're going to Baltimore," Jimmy measured his words, and read aright the sudden flash of desperation in the captain's eyes.

"Quartermaster, give me a hand!" Bankhead shouted—but before he could draw his gun, Jimmy Christopher's fist came up in a pile-driving blow to the point of his jaw.

Jimmy whirled, even before the captain's body had hit the deck—to confront the quartermaster. But that seaman eyed him with grim approval and then turned back to the wheel.

"The course is southwest, to Baltimore, Quartermaster," Jimmy repeated his command, and the helmsman's head nodded. "Aye, aye, sir—south by southeast it is," he answered, and the wheel twirled, to swing the big liner away from New York....

Half a dozen times that night, the mutineers attacked the bridge, but every time Jimmy and his men, backed by the loyal officers, drove them off. Tim was having his troubles in the engine-room, too. Jimmy heard the sound of shots coming over the wire to the bridge, but Tim was holding his own, and the engines continued to turn.

Through the night hours, and then through the gray of morning, they held those posts while a ship full of mutineers snarled and spat their hate. Eleven o'clock, twelve, one… and the *Imperator* was sailing up the Chesapeake. Jimmy knew that it was useless to try to pick up a pilot—the mutineers would not let a pilot come aboard.

Carefully her officers picked their way through the unfamiliar channel. Now Baltimore lay right ahead, the *Imperator* nosing its way into the harbor—when a terrific concussion shook the vessel from stem to stern. Quickly Jimmy grabbed the engine-room telegraph, but there was no answer to his anxious calls.

Something was the matter down there! He had to know what; had to find out, if he must fight his way through the whole crew to do so. Gun in hand, he threw open the bridge door— and caught the sound of firing, saw the mutineers running in panic. And then Tim Donovan and Carey ran up, half-carrying Rockwell.

"They had dynamite!" Tim gasped. "Harry Walton saw them—but he was too late. He jumped right down on top of them—was blown to pieces. We're sinking, Jimmy—the engine-room is filling up. We'll go down at any minute!"

# CHAPTER 12
# THE BULLET-SHEDDERS

THE *IMPERATOR* sank in the middle of Baltimore harbor, but a host of shore boats surrounded her when she went down. Jimmy Christopher and Tim managed to get the wounded Rockwell onto a tug, and Tully and Faroni clambered up after them. Stepping into the captain's cabin, Jimmy quickly identified himself and asked that the tug take him to a pier immediately.

"Gladly, Operator 5." The grizzled captain saluted respectfully. "And thank God that you've come, sir. But it doesn't look as if any human aid can help America now—not the way this New Dawn is sweeping right on."

"They aren't threatening Baltimore yet, are they, Captain?" Jimmy wanted to know.

"Depends on what you call 'threatening,'" the graybeard grunted. "They aren't marching into the city yet, but it looks like that won't be long coming. We stand in the way of Washington—there isn't much doubt that we'll get our share."

The moment he landed, Jimmy saw that the captain was not the only one who feared the worst. The city had a bad case of the jitters. Anxious-eyed people greeted him on every side, and already the exodus of refugees had begun. Cars, loaded with household goods, were heading in the direction of Washington—away from the gathering storm.

Most of those refugees did not stop in the capital, for the panic there was even greater than in Baltimore. Already Washington seemed half deserted, and the rest of the population poised to flee at a moment's notice. Not only the civilian population, but the government officials as well. Before Jimmy had been in the city an hour he felt that the Federal government was tottering. It needed only the approach of the New Dawn forces to send it down in utter collapse.

"There is no confidence, Jimmy," President Warren admitted, when Jimmy was admitted to his study and had been held tight in the sturdy old New Englander's embrace. "It isn't that our men are afraid. It is more than that—it's as if they realize that there is no use fighting against the inevitable. Against ordinary troops we could hold our own—we proved that at Santa Fe. But this is something different. This is demoralizing, morale-shattering. You can't blame a man for falling back when he knows that his weapons are useless against the oncoming enemy."

"That's what I want to know about," Jimmy picked up quickly. "What is this hocus-pocus about deathless men?"

"I only wish it were hocus-pocus Jimmy," Warren sighed. "Unfortunately, it is more than that—impossible as the idea may seem. Our best observers have come back with the same reports. These shock troops of the New Dawn's are able to shed bullets as if they were no more than ordinary hail. I know—the obvious answer is armor. That could protect a man's body, but the trouble with armor always has been that it leaves a man's face vulnerable. But not these men, Jimmy—their faces shed bullets just as effectively as the rest of their bodies! You can't blame the troops for dubbing them 'deathless men' and considering them impregnable."

Men who could walk through a wave of bullets—men who could laugh at the leaden death-messengers, that splashed into their faces.... Such a thing was inconceivable, and yet Jimmy had too much respect for Andrew Warren's well balanced judgment to doubt the truth of what he was hearing.

Still, there must be an answer to this miracle-working—and if America was to be saved that solution *must* be found.

"General Morgan did his utmost to hold Philadelphia, but a rebellion broke out behind his back, in the city itself," Warren was reviewing the gloomy succession of defeats that had brought America to its knees. "The press has been howling for Morgan's scalp, but there is no use removing him. He is doing all that any man could do—and it was only masterly strategy that enabled him to preserve his army when that Philadelphia trap closed on them. He managed to keep his men together, and fell back— yesterday he had to yield Wilmington. Next it will be Baltimore—and then Washington. We will still fight on after that, but with the capital in the hands of the New Dawn...."

Jimmy Christopher knew well enough what that would mean. Grimly he resolved that, miracles or no miracles, the on-sweeping tide must be stopped before it reached the shore of the Potomac.

"I'm going up to have a talk with Morgan," he decided quickly. "Maybe he can tell me something more about these deathless men. Perhaps I can even get a look at one of them."

That jerked Andrew Warren out of the gloomy abstraction that had enveloped him. Quickly he looked up and eyed Jimmy keenly, inquiringly.

150

"If there is anyone who can find the solution to this thing, you are the man, Jimmy," he admitted. "God knows we need that solution—in a hurry, if it is to do us any good. But don't take any unnecessary chances. You can't risk a clash with these storm troopers—that will only mean your death. We need you, Jimmy—America and I."

Thoughtfully, he watched Jimmy Christopher turn and stride from the office. There was something stirring behind that tense, inscrutable face, some plan forming in that agile brain—Warren sensed that. But had he known what Jimmy Christopher contemplated he never would have permitted his undercover ace to leave the Executive Mansion....

GENERAL HORATIO MORGAN had drawn up his nearly demoralized army along the southern bank of the Susquehanna River—the last natural boundary that separated the on-coming New Dawn host from Baltimore and then Washington. A beaten, morale-shattered force, Jimmy Christopher walked down their lines and inspected their hastily erected breastworks and entrenchments. In every face he read incipient panic and rout. These men knew that they were about to face a foe with whom they could not hope to cope. They were not afraid to die, yet were beaten before the first gun was fired.

"I know what you see—inevitable defeat," Morgan nodded. "It is their shock troops, Operator 5—they are uncanny. I have seen them walk straight into machine-gun fire that should have mowed them down in rows. Sometimes they fell, yes—or were knocked down. But they got up again, and came on as if nothing had happened! What can we do against men like that? We haven't enough cannon to blow them all to pieces with shells. Yet that is about all that seems to stop them."

"They can be stopped, General—and we are *going* to stop them!" Jimmy said. He proceeded to outline the plan that had been forming in his mind—the plan on which he must stake the fate of America. "We'll try to hold them across the Susquehanna, of course," he finished, "but, if they manage to ford the river, my plan goes into effect. And now, first of all, I want to speak to the troops."

Mounted on a gun carriage, Operator 5 talked to those men who had seen defeat on a dozen battlefields, who had watched helplessly while anarchy and ruination swept over the country. Listlessly they gathered around for what, they felt, was to be another useless pep talk. But as word of Jimmy's identity spread through the ranks new hope kindled in many. More than once, Operator 5 had saved America when all hope was past. Was it possible that, once more, he could snatch victory from defeat—that he could offer some plan to offset the devilish advantage of the deathless men?

"There is nothing supernatural about these storm troopers," he told them quietly. "You all know that. They are hiding behind some new weapon they have developed. This cowardly weapon allows them to commit murder without risking their own lives. I am going to discover what it is. I shall find a way to defeat it—I promise you that."

He finished, "All I ask is that you stand firm for a few days more. Face these renegades as American soldiers have faced the enemy since the days of 1775. I am asking you to do nothing that I will not do myself. I shall be with you tomorrow when you face these 'deathless men'. I'll lead you when we charge them."

Slowly that indefinable something that made Jimmy Christopher different from other men began to have its effect upon them. His tremendous personal magnetism reached out, gripped them, inspiring new confidence and rekindling the will to win in their hearts. Their cheers rang out with new fervor, when he had finished. Defiantly that cheering swept over the Susquehanna to where the host of the New Dawn were preparing for the morrow.

In the morning it was a newly inspired American army that crouched in the trenches and stood ready to meet the long-dreaded assault.

GENERAL WLADEK RIEGEL lost no time resuming the offensive. With Philadelphia, Camden and Wilmington at his back, he was impatient to push on to Baltimore and Washington—and also contemptuous of the defeated, discouraged army that stood in his way. His yellow-uniformed engineers marched to the river-bank and began the construction of the pontoon bridge that would span the Susquehanna. As the work progressed steadily, and the out-thrusting end of the bridge came closer and closer to the southern shore, the fire from the American lines became heavier and heavier. Through his field glasses, Jimmy could see it dotting the water with splashes like heavy raindrops could see it pecking splinters from the boats and the planks that were laid over them, stabbing at the busy builders—and apparently causing them not the slightest discomfort! Only when one of the big guns made a direct hit on the

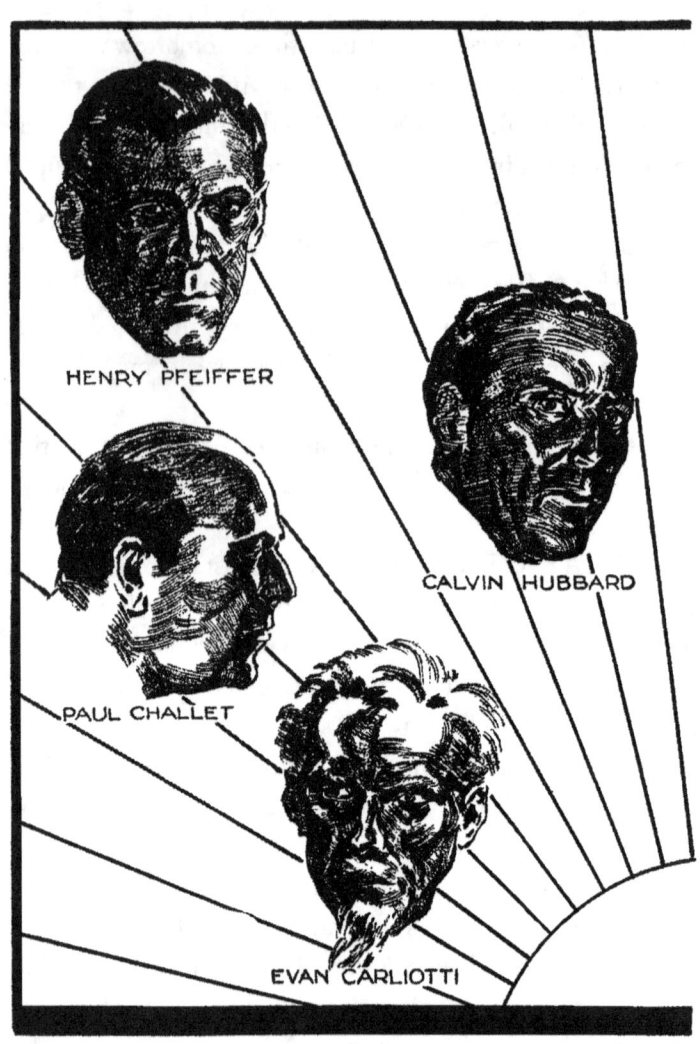

HENRY PFEIFFER

CALVIN HUBBARD

PAUL CHALLET

EVAN CARLIOTTI

154

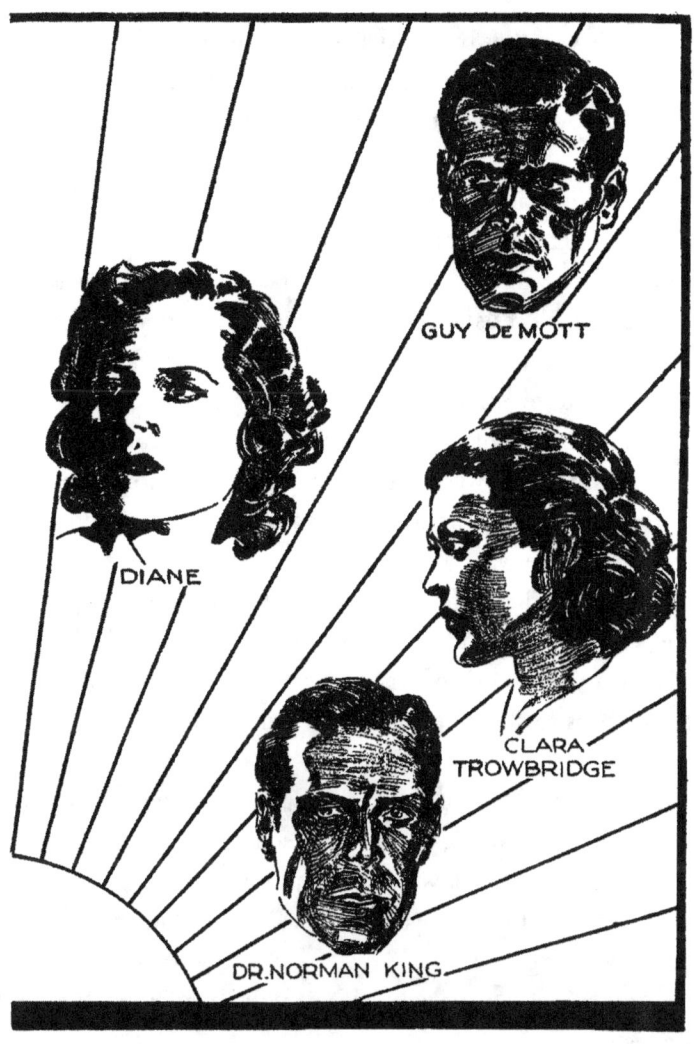

pontoons was that bridge delayed. But General Morgan had little artillery, and, in the general confusion that had enveloped Washington, most of the shells he had received were of the wrong size.

Now four enemy bridges were creeping out over the river. Closer, closer they came. The first reached the farther shore, and waves of the vaunted shock troops came pouring across them, bayoneting all resistance out of their way as they cleared the shore right up to the line of the American trenches.

It was an incredible thing Jimmy was now beholding—an army forming ranks in the face of withering machine-gun and rifle fire. That was what those New Dawn storm troopers were doing! Unhurriedly, they formed their lines, then came on, charging in wave after wave of irresistible force. Men who could not be killed! Men who went down but got right up again and came on, unharmed as if no bullet had even touched them! Men who walked through death and clambered up over the trench tops to slaughter the helpless defenders with bayonets and grenades!

Human flesh could not stand up against such an unholy onslaught. The American lines cracked and broke. The trenches were lost, and the yellow horde swept forward inexorably.

"Now it has to be my way, General," Jimmy said quietly, as he laid down his glasses.

"You have seen for yourself—it will be suicide!" Morgan protested.

But Operator 5 had already gone.

Racing across the field in the face of the oncoming rout,

Jimmy shouted to the fleeing soldiers. A few rallied, joined him—enough to make a storming party that could gather behind a low knoll and then charge into the oncoming storm troopers.

That gallant suicide company did not even make the "deathless men" break their stride. Straight on the yellow-garbed attackers came, their bullets and bayonets clearing the way with machinelike thoroughness. Desperately Jimmy's volunteers fought their way up to the enemy line with him—but there they went down, one after the other....

And Jimmy Christopher went down with them!

Sprawled flat on his face, he lay there as the New Dawn waves swept over him and pressed on to the utter rout of Morgan's decimated regiments.

At any moment Jimmy expected to feel the downward thrust of the bayonet that would end his life, or the blasting pain of a bullet crashing into his brain. But the shock troopers had no time for wounded men, or to see whether or not those who went down were dead.

It was the desperate gamble Jimmy had taken....

Lying there, he lifted his head guardedly. Some fifty feet from him, was what he sought—a New Dawn storm trooper who had been knocked down. The fellow was getting to his feet, shaking his head as if to clear it. But before he could get started again and catch up with his companions, Jimmy Christopher was upon him.

With all his strength Jimmy brought his automatic down on the fellow's skull—again and again, until the "deathless one's" knees buckled and he slipped to the ground in an inert heap. Quickly Jimmy crouched beside him. He dragged the senseless trooper to the shelter of a clump of shrubbery and pushed him in beneath the foliage.

Disarming his prisoner, Jimmy tied his wrists together and then waited until he returned to consciousness.

"One sound out of you and you are a dead man!" Jimmy warned, as the automatic jabbed into the fellow's ribs. But those blows over the head seemed to have taken all thought of resistance out of the trooper. He lay like a dummy, yellow-faced, hollow-eyed. He lay there, uncomplaining, all day and then, when night had fallen, got to his feet when Jimmy commanded it.

Warily Jimmy led the way over the dark countryside, alert for a meeting with New Dawn troopers or stragglers. But the way was clear almost up to the lines. Docilely the captive trudged along at his side and then meekly submitted to being tied to a tree.

Leaving him there, Jimmy crept forward several hundred yards. He took out a flare carried in his pocket, set it on the ground and touched a match to it. He raced back into the darkness, the moment its rocket popped into the air and was followed by a blinding burst of light.

Now if Horatio Morgan was only ready to do his part....

Jimmy wondered.

General Morgan was ready. Even before that flare had died, the American guns began to bark and the astonished New Dawners were amazed to see a raiding column come charging down upon them. So unexpected was that surprising maneuver that the rebel lines gave way, were pushed back under the onslaught—back until they were beyond the clump of straggly trees where Jimmy Christopher crouched beside his precious prisoner.

He waited.

Wladek Riegel never did understand that senseless raid that cost scores of American lives and gained nothing—nothing at all. His men reformed their lines immediately, and, in a few minutes, they had swept back across the ground just lost. A senseless raid, but little did he suspect what had actually happened during those few minutes. For when Operator 5 slipped safely behind the American lines, he took with him a prisoner. That prisoner carried on his person the secret Evan Carliotti would have protected had it cost him a score of army corps!

ONCE JIMMY CHRISTOPHER reached General Morgan's headquarters the way was clear. Already warmed up, a swift Army pursuit plane stood ready to speed him and his captive to Washington. He radioed Dr. Norman King to hold himself in readiness for their arrival.

Norman King was ready, pacing the floor of his laboratory impatiently when Jimmy hurried in, leading his captive.

"There he is, Doc," Jimmy said. "One of the 'deathless men'. I got him for you as I said I would—now tell me what makes him work."

"Dope, first of all," King diagnosed, as he seated the trooper in a chair and looked into his eyes. "This fellow is so doped up that he is practically insensible to pain. Dope, and chain metal." He opened the fellow's yellow tunic and examined the close-meshed steel chain armor that lined it. "Mighty fine work, this—strong enough to stop any machine-gun bullet. With flesh insensible to the pounding, and this armor to shed the bullets the storm trooper would be quite impervious to a hail of lead.

"But here is something else!" the doctor whistled in surprise, as he bent close over the captive. "This stuff on his face and hands! Have you seen *this*, Operator 5?"

Jimmy bent over beside him. He stared in amazement as Norman King's supple fingers worked up along the fellow's neck and started to peel the very skin from it! That was what it looked like. But Jimmy soon saw that what came loose was a thin mask—a yellow outer covering that clung to the skin of his hands and face like another layer of epidermis! The trooper's head was entirely covered by this, wherever it was not protected by his chain metal-lined cap. His hands were encased in regular mittens.

"Some sort of silk!" Norman King whistled again as he examined the mask beneath a strong light. "Stuff with a silk base. I remember now," he recalled. "I read some time ago about an ancient Japanese silk developed to the point where it was strong as any armor. This must be the same sort of treatment. But these New Dawn inventors have added to it, perfected it so that, instead of being stiff and hard, it is supple and form-fitting. No wonder it does no good to shoot these fellows in the face—they wear bullet-proof masks!"

He went on. "And that reminds me of something else." King's

eyes narrowed and the little muscles at the corners of his jaws bunched out. "Lawrence, my assistant who was murdered here in the laboratory, had a mania for silks. He was always experimenting with them. That's why he was killed!" His eyes flashed suddenly. "That's why the laboratory was burned so as to make it appear that all his notes and papers were destroyed. They were stolen—and this no doubt is the result of that theft!"

"And the weapon that will mean the downfall of America unless we find some way to counteract it," Jimmy added solemnly. "We've *got* to find a way to penetrate this stuff, Doc. As long as these masks remain bullet-proof, the New Dawn troopers will be invincible. We've *got* to find the answer before Wladek Riegel is able to take Washington. That gives us mighty little time. Baltimore is already in his grip. It will fall tomorrow, and the day after that the New Dawn will march into Washington."

For hours Norman King treated that mask and those gloves with every chemical that came into his mind. He wet the silk preparation, heated it, froze it, tried to burn it—but nothing diminished its tough resiliency. Far into the night he and Jimmy racked their brains trying to find some way to make it penetrable—and the result was failure.

"If I could only discover what they use in preparing the stuff," King moaned, "perhaps I could tear it down and attack it in that way. But there is nothing to give us an inkling—nothing that gives us the slightest hint...."

His words faded into futility, lost in the silence that pressed in upon them as they looked at each other and confessed that they were beaten. Silence so heavy that it seemed to be alive with unseen eyes, unseen ears and….

Suddenly Jimmy's head jerked erect, listening. He had heard the sound of a muffled footstep. But even the memory of that faint sound was blotted out by the crash of glass and the terrific explosion that followed. The explosion seemed to rend the whole world into little pieces and bring them raining down on his head—until he was stifling, was suffocating beneath them….

Blindly Jimmy groped his way up out of that avalanche, fumbled around in the dark laboratory. The acrid stench of burned cordite filled his nostrils, and the noise of tumbling, crunching wreckage filled his ears when he moved. He took out the emergency flashlight he always carried clipped to an inside pocket, snapped it on—and turned its beam on the litter around him.

The laboratory was completely wrecked, Jimmy saw that at a glance. Chairs and tables were overturned, bottles tossed from shelves, expensive scientific equipment lay piled in ruins… and out from under one of those piles crawled Dr. Norman King.

Groggily he got to his feet and stared open-mouthed. Not at his wrecked laboratory, but at a broken bottle that lay overturned on one of the shelves. Its contents had spilled over the shelf and a trickle was dripping over one edge—dripping down onto the silk mask that lay beneath it.

That mask was fizzing, smoking—*was bursting into flames!*

"That's it!" King yelled wildly. "There it is, Jimmy! The dirty rat who tried to blow us to pieces has solved our problem!"

## CHAPTER 13
## LAST STAND

"WHERE IS Diane Elliot? Has there been no word from here?" Those were the first questions Jimmy Christopher had demanded of his father and of President Warren as soon as he reached Washington on his return from Europe. But both had given him the same reluctant answer—had pointed to Honesdale, in the very center of the New Dawn occupied territory.

"That is where she was when she was last heard from—when Tim saw her warning beacon," John Christopher said gently. "She may be all right there, Jimmy. I have tried to get word to her, to reach her with out best men. But that town is guarded like the Sub-Treasury. Perhaps that is why they are holding her—so that she cannot divulge whatever she may have discovered."

But the New Dawn was no longer holding Diane in Honesdale, nor even in Pittsburgh. She had gone far beyond that, trailing with the camp-followers in the rear of the victorious storm-troop-led army.

Through Harrisburg and Reading, through looted Philadelphia and Camden, through Wilmington and to the threshold of Baltimore she followed them. Daily, hourly, her rage and horror increased as she saw the destruction these wanton destroyers were wreaking. The work of reconstruction, that Jimmy Christopher had pushed so tirelessly, was being torn down and laid waste on every hand.

A score of times she had tried to get through the New Dawn

lines and reach General Morgan. But always she had failed. Alert sentries had barred her way, turned her back from whence she had come. Half a dozen disguises and excuses she had used, but all had failed miserably. Yet there *must* be some way that she could escape and reach Andrew Warren before it was too late.

Daily she had to witness the triumphant advance of these "deathless men"—and she *knew* the secret of their immunity to bullets. Sewed into the hem of her dress she carried the sample of the silklike preparation that protected them....

Then she saw the call for experienced nurses posted in captured Wilmington. Here was a way, at least, of getting up near the front lines. Afterward she might have a chance to get into a wounded soldier's uniform and charge into General Morgan's wavering lines!

Diane took her place in the line of applicants, and again that day destiny seemed to pick her out.

As she stood there waiting her turn to be interviewed, a familiar figure strode across the reception room, and a cold chill trickled down her back. He turned, and a frigid grip closed around her heart. There was no mistake. It was Henry Pfeiffer, perfectly at home here in the New Dawn medical headquarters!

And then he saw her.

Instantly she saw recognition flare in his eyes, but abruptly he turned and left the room. What did that mean? Had he gone to inform against her, to have her arrested as a spy? Diane tensed. But in a few moments he was back with a sheaf of forms in his hand, asking her name, experience.

"I think we can use you, Miss Mosby." He nodded. "Please step this way," and led the way to a side office.

Diane followed, wondering what game the man could be playing. But the moment the door closed behind them, he turned and grinned at her.

"How is my patient?" he laughed. "Lots of water has flowed under the bridge since then, hasn't it, Diane Elliot? I've wondered a lot about you—whether you were able to make your way back to Washington after you escaped from the Honesdale jail. I knew you were there, of course, but there was nothing I could do for you. I walked on eggs myself in that town, and I have not been a lot safer since."

"Have you gotten word back to Washington—to Andrew Warren or Secretary Hubbard?" Diane asked, as she tried to read the riddle that was Henry Pfeiffer.

"Tried to get word through by two men—and each ended up in front of a firing-squad," he told her. "But you're trying to get through now—that's why you want this nurse job," he suddenly divined. "I can get you through quicker than that—tonight, if you're ready. My plans are completed—motorcycle cached and arrangements all made. You can come with me if you will ride the back seat."

Through the New Dawn lines that night! If she could manage that she might be able to reach President Warren with her information in time to save Washington!

Diane's pulses leaped. She did not trust Henry Pfeiffer—but she would ride behind the Devil himself, dash through hell with him, if that would get her into Washington! Eagerly she agreed,

One of these devils bent down and ignited the pile of fagots at their feet!

listened intently as he gave his directions, and when she left him his parting admonition was ringing in her ears:

"Eight o'clock—on the dot—and I'll have you in Washington before midnight!"

**LIKE HUNGRY** wolves Wladek Riegel's New Dawn army closed in on Baltimore and swept the defending forces out of its path. Irresistibly his deathless legions marched up to the muzzles of blazing machine-guns and bayoneted the hapless gunners. Miles to the south, in a Washington laboratory, Operator 5 labored with Dr. Norman King and a score of assistants, risking their very lives, in a frantic effort to produce a potent preparation on which depended the fate of America.

General Morgan's lines broke in the face of that enemy charge, as he knew they must—broke and streamed back toward Washington in complete disorder. Had Riegel pursued his advantage that day, the history of America might have been written far differently.

But no sooner had his rabble army swarmed into the fallen city than they went wild.

For twenty-four hours Baltimore was raped and pillaged. While its finest citizens suffered their martyrdom, Horatio Morgan struggled mightily to reform his shattered lines. At last he managed to stem the rout and dig in for a last stand on the west bank of the Patuxent River. The on-rushing New Dawn horde would have no difficulty fording that stream, he knew—but he was obeying orders. Operator 5 had begged him to battle for every hour, every minute, that he could possibly hold out. Now those hours were bound to be very few....

Operator 5 had promised to be on hand in the morning to help meet that last onslaught, and he arrived promptly. He came with a fleet of curious little trucks that were like street cleaners' handcarts. These trucks were carefully entrenched in a series of little pillboxes that had been hastily constructed for them half a mile back from the river.

"Let the enemy ford the river," Jimmy directed grimly as he laid out the plan for this last-ditch defense with Morgan and his staff, "Let them get a good foothold on his bank. I want them to come marching up in their full strength. When they are almost to the trenches, we will charge them—and then fall back beyond the pillboxes, apparently in the usual route. But at the pillboxes we stand. There we wipe out the New Dawn—or die!"

EARLY THAT fatal morning the march on Washington began. Contemptuously the New Dawn engineers spanned the narrow Patuxent, and the yellow-uniformed legions swarmed over to its western bank—where less than twenty miles of level, undefendable country lay between them and the nation's capitol. Straight into the blasting fire of the entrenched defenders, the shock troopers marched—but this time there was a variation in their usual tactics, that variation Jimmy Christopher was quick to note.

Through field glasses, he peered at the advancing line—fearful of some unexpected ruse. Unbelievingly he stared—then stared again. Up there in front of the foremost line came a white horse—in its saddle the almost naked body of a girl! Her chestnut-crowned head was bent forward. Jimmy clamped the glasses with knuckle-whitened fingers, red rage seething in his brain. *That girl was Diane Elliot!*

Her face was fearlessly turned to the guns that must send her to death. Helpless, her legs were tied to the stirrups, wrists lashed to the pommel of the saddle.

General Morgan saw that pitiful figure at the same moment, and must have recognized her as well. His glasses came down from his eyes.

"We can't…" he started to say; but Jimmy Christopher took the words out of his mouth.

"We're charging!" he rasped. *"Now!"* And then he was over the top, zigzagging a crazy course toward that oncoming horse and its doomed rider. Beside him came the defending troops, yelling like madmen—but Jimmy scarcely saw them or heard their cheers. He had eyes only for a white, stricken face that bobbed above a white charger—ears only for the words he could almost see trembling on her lips.

Now she was no more than fifty feet away… twenty-five—and then he was clutching for the horse's bridle, just as the splendid animal squealed in agony and dropped, killed by half a dozen bullets even before it reached the earth. Jimmy tried to spring clear as the horse pitched forward, but he did not make it. The lurching animal knocked him down, pinned him there by one leg. Frantically Jimmy tried to tear himself free, to reach the girl—only to find her now thrown almost on top of him.

"Diane!" he gasped, and then an amazing relief surged through him—a relief tinged with wonder.

She was not Diane—but *Clara Trowbridge!* Clara Trowbridge

deliberately made-up to resemble Diane from a distance, but not sufficiently well to deceive anyone at close range. Clara Trowbridge, whom he thought somewhere in France; there on the battlefield disguised as Diane! This was the sort of fantasy of which nightmares are made. It didn't make sense....

"Clara," he began half-hesitantly.

But she understood. A pain-tightened smile etched her lips as she clutched at her breast with a blood-dripping hand. "Yes, Operator 5," she gasped. "Clara Trowbridge, who should have died in France—and is going to die in America instead. No," she objected as he tried to move, tried to prevent her from sheltering him with her own body. "Stay there where you are—please! I am hit—badly. I haven't much time. I want to talk—just like any woman...."

The blood was pouring out of her chest, soaking her whole side, and Jimmy saw that there was little anyone could do for her. Her time was short, and the knowledge seemed to make her panicky.

"I am a traitor, Operator 5," she rushed on as she fought for breath. "Betraying people has always—been my business. I was a spy of Evan Carliotti's, here in American—before I married Larry. That was why I married him, why I made him fall in love with me—because I knew that he was one of your most trusted men. Carliotti wanted to know everything that you were doing, wanted me to watch on you."

She faltered on. "I betrayed your men—led them into traps for Carliotti's killers. Then Larry walked into one himself. At first, that wouldn't have mattered—but I had fallen in love with him, Operator 5—I would have given my own life for him. But Carliotti's killers shot him down."

She shuddered. "I blamed you for that—and followed you all over France. I trailed you there to Charnay and notified Carliotti. I saw you step out of that trap and escape to England, and reported you again—to the London headquarters. I thought that had finished you. Then I realized that it was not you, that it was I—I who had killed Larry with my duplicity and double-crossing."

Her face softened. "He never suspected me, Operator 5—never thought that I was anything but a loyal American. All of a sudden I realized that was what I wanted to be. I had not lived like one, but I could die the sort of woman he had believed me. So I came back to America. I had little trouble working myself into the confidence of the New Dawn leaders. I learned all their plans—about the armament these deathless men wear. But I could not get back to you with my information."

Her voice shook. "I knew you were here—with the government forces. Riegel knew it, too, and offered a reward for your head. That gave me my inspiration. I know Riegel—and how he would treat Diane Elliot if he ever laid his hands on her. So I disguised myself as Diane and had myself caught. Riegel did just what I knew he would. He sent me out here like this—to be your welcoming committee—to be killed before your eyes."

Clara Trowbridge's face was a ghastly bluish-white, her voice a mere whisper.

But she clung to life until her confession was made—sufficiently long to gasp out revelations that filled Operator 5 with burning rage for the unsuspected man who had stabbed him in the back.

Then Clara Trowbridge died as her Larry had always believed she lived, a loyal American woman willing and glad to make the supreme sacrifice for her country....

Gently Jimmy pushed the limp body aside and tugged at his imprisoned leg until it was free. The New Dawn horde had long since swept over him, and the battlefront had moved back—now almost to that line of hidden pillboxes!

FOLLOWING OPERATOR 5'S orders, the defenders had fallen back, fleeing in what seemed an utter rout, when they had crushed against the unyielding wall of the deathless ones. Running *wildly*, they made no attempt to defend their trenches, scrambling over them for their lives in the race toward Washington. Behind them came the New Dawn phalanx, confident, arrogant—the deathless ones who had nothing to fear from the bullets.

Washington was less than twenty miles!

Jeering at their fleeing foes, they swept on—until suddenly the sloping ground in front of them was pitted by what seemed to be puffs of smoke rising from a dozen different points. Those puffs leaped up in front of them, reached out tenuous fingers, clutched at their faces and made them burn fiercely—*suddenly bursting them into flames!*

A wave of men with flaming hands and faces! And then the whitish smoke had reached the second line, the third. And the flames were spreading, turning that victorious legion into a tortured mob of blazing men, who screamed in awful agony

173

as they flung themselves on the ground, rolling and threshing vainly in a hopeless struggle to smother the fire that was now searing them to death!

Sick with horror, Jimmy Christopher turned away from that ghastly spectacle. The reorganized American troops came charging into the suffering ranks and completed the destruction of the cream of the New Dawn army. In utter rout the rabble that followed in the wake of the storm troopers turned and fled for their lives… and the threat to Washington was ended.

The Capitol was saved from the deathless horde. But as Operator 5 sped back to it he knew that his work was not finished.

The New Dawn was not yet dead while its vicious head remained alive to sink his poisonous fangs into the unsuspecting back of America!

DIANE ELLIOT expected to be seized and arrested at any moment as she crouched in a black-arched doorway and cast anxious glances up and down Wilmington's Sheridan Avenue. The looting and rioting had passed and the Delaware city was now like a place of the dead, apparently tenanted only by swaggering New Dawn troopers.

As she listened, Diane caught the sound for which she waited. The muffled popping of a motorcycle came closer, closer. With a tinkle and wheezing of machinery Henry Pfeiffer rounded a dark corner and was in front of her, inviting her to the seat behind him—offering her a strap to secure herself for the wild ride ahead.

Then they were roaring on their way.

Henry Pfeiffer glided up to the outposts with supreme

unconcern. Confidently he handed over his papers, and in a few moments they were respectfully waved on their way.

Pfeiffer had kept his word, had gotten her clear of New Dawn territory. But as she clung to his back, and the machine raced through the cool night air, Diane told herself again that there was something off-color about this man. The way those officers had saluted him—the sly, knowing looks given him—hinted at a closer understanding than even the cleverest spy would have been able to establish with the enemy.

Back into Diane's mind flashed memories of Honesdale, of the *coup* that had failed, of the ease with which Henry Pfeiffer had shucked his role of doctor to blossom forth as one of the New Dawn leaders. Damningly suspicious circumstances, they only added to her inherent distrust of the man. She was under some obligation to him, she admitted, but her first obligation was to America, no matter what steps that might necessitate. Firmly, she determined that she would do her duty and imme- diately declare her suspicions of Henry Pfeiffer.

Pfeiffer was as good as his word. He delivered her in Wash- ington long before midnight.

He drove her straight to a side door of the War Department Building before he stopped the machine.

"Secretary Hubbard is expecting me," he explained. "We'll see him first, and then I will be at your service."

Diane would have preferred to have gone directly to the President, but perhaps Secretary Hubbard would be better for the unpleasant task that lay before her. Hubbard was Henry

Pfeiffer's superior and should be the first to learn of his man's activities....

**SECRETARY CALVIN HUBBARD** was waiting for them in his private office. He greeted them warmly and then sat back to listen while Henry Pfeiffer made his report, giving an accurate account of conditions behind the New Dawn lines and a description of the process whereby Wladek Riegel's storm troopers were made invulnerable.

"So that is it," Hubbard marveled. "In the morning we'll start our laboratories to work on that. But now, Miss Elliot, is there anything you may wish to add to Captain Pfeiffer's report?"

"Yes, Mr. Secretary, there is," Diane's voice was calm and measured and her eyes gazed fearlessly into Pfeiffer's. "I believe this man is a traitor. I believe he is tricking you, pretending to be one of your operatives while he actually is a leader of the New Dawn!"

Calvin Hubbard's eyes saucered with surprise, and he opened his mouth as if he intended to speak, to protest. But Diane went right on, outlining her suspicions, narrating what she had seen and heard, making point after point that Henry Pfeiffer would find it difficult to answer. As she spoke, she saw that her words were having little effect on the Secretary. He was shaking his head, patronizing disbelief was plain on his face. "You are wrought up, Miss Elliot—in a nervous state where anything looks highly suspicious to you," he tried to calm her. "That is easily understandable, after what you have been through. But I have implicit confidence in Captain Pfeiffer. The role he has played with the New Dawn is just what he planned when he penetrated their lines."

But it wasn't—couldn't be. Diane had seen and heard sufficient to *know* that there was more to Pfeiffer's activity than that. Still, she could make no impression on the Secretary.

"I give you notice that I shall repeat these charges to President Warren," she gave up as she saw that he wished to terminate the interview.

"As you wish, Miss Elliot," Hubbard bowed, "but first perhaps I can convince you that you are wrong. At the present moment we are detaining a person in this building who may be able to reveal things which will surprise you. Come with me where you can see and hear for yourself." Diane passed Henry Pfeiffer as she followed the Secretary from the room, and for a moment her eyes clashed with the spy's—clashed and sent an electric tingle through her body. It was not that Pfeiffer's eyes were hostile. They were jeering, triumphant—the eyes of a man who laughs at a vanquished antagonist.

Calvin Hubbard led the way downstairs to a corridor of little rooms that probably were used for storage purposes. At one of these doors he stopped and drew a clasp of keys from his pocket, opened the door and then switched on the light inside.

"There, Miss Elliot," he waved his hand invitingly to the doorway. "Perhaps you will recognize Jim—"

Jimmy Christopher! Involuntarily Diane took a startled step into that doorway—and then she realized her mistake. With a sudden shove she was pushed into the room, sent reeling across it, and the door closed and locked behind her. An empty room, furnished only with an army cot and a pitcher of water—a prison cell from which she saw at once it would be absolutely impossible to escape!

So Henry Pfeiffer *was* a traitor—working hand in glove with Calvin Hubbard! It was astounding, but no other conclusion could she reach. Calvin Hubbard was a traitor, a schemer who plotted to overthrow the government and then ride in on the crest of the New Dawn!

Now she had the real secret of the uprising in the palm of her hand. But she was more helpless than if she had been miles behind those New Dawn lines through which she had so frantically penetrated....

Hardly glancing up when a stony-faced guard brought her food and fresh water, Diane sat there in her cell.... A day passed, and then another had gone well past noon before she had a visitor.

That visitor was Henry Pfeiffer, and at a glance she saw that all his sardonic insouciance had left him. He was excited, anxious-eyed and, for once, was candidly frank.

"You are pretty keen, Diane Elliot," he admitted. "I recognized that the first time I saw you. That was why I went to such pains to cover myself—just in case I should later need you as an alibi. It seems, now, that that will not be necessary. But you may still prove to be my ace in the hole. Come along—I think I'll play you now and see."

A helpless pawn in that traitors' game, Diane got up when he grabbed her by the wrist. She let him lead her to she knew not what....

SPEED WAS what Operator 5 wanted most of all as he raced toward Washington in an Army car commandeered at General Morgan's headquarters. He pressed the machine to its utmost speed, while Clara Trowbridge's dying revelations throbbed through his brain. He should be in Washington at that very moment. Perhaps already he was too late—for once the news of the New Dawn debacle reached the capitol he knew that desperation would dictate and all pretense would be cast aside.

Once the traitors who had planned to throttle America knew that they were defeated, God only knew what would happen!

The Capitol seemed as usual when he sped through the outskirts and entered the city proper. But he would feel no assurance or guarantee, until he reached Andrew Warren and saw that the President was safe—until the traitorous snake, now hiding in the Chief Executive's official family, had been dragged into the open and scotched....

Jimmy's persistent fear was realized the moment he dashed up to the White House steps and was met by one of Warren's private secretaries. The President? He had gone to the War Department Building some time ago in response to an urgent call from Secretary Hubbard.

Secretary Hubbard! Into Jimmy's mind flashed the memory of another occasion when Andrew Warren had hurried to the War Department Building in answer to an urgent call from his Secretary. Jimmy remembered what they had found there. His teeth gritted as he realized that he had stood shoulder to shoulder in that wrecked laboratory with the man who was responsible for Graham Lawrence's murder. This same monster had now called the unsuspecting President of the United States to his office!

Jimmy hurriedly covered the distance to the War Department Building, and the moment he entered he saw that something was wrong. No guards were at the doors, the corridors were deserted—and Secretary Hubbard's office was empty. The big stone building was as silent as a mausoleum. But Jimmy set the echoes ringing as he sprinted down the stairs and pounded his way along the lower corridor to Norman King's laboratory. A score of men still were working day and night to produce the chemical spray that had ended the reign of the deathless men.

The laboratory where a score of men should have been working…. Jimmy saw that the place was a shambles. His recent comrades lay sprawled over their work tables, slumped on the floor, flung in every direction. The Grim Reaper had visited this laboratory and sprayed it from end to end with leaden death!

The heavy stillness of a morgue was on the place—until one of those blood-splashed figures moved and crawled out from behind a work table. Norman King! Jimmy was kneeling at his side in a moment, opening his shirt and doing his best to ease the wounded man's breathing. King's eyes were only half-open, but he was coming back to his senses, fighting his way to consciousness… and in a moment he recognized Jimmy.

"The President!" he gasped. "Those devils have him! Downstairs, I think. Don't bother about me, Jimmy—I don't matter. But for God's sake, find Andy Warren before it's too late! Tim Donovan—"

But Jimmy Christopher waited to hear no more. Andrew

Warren was a captive somewhere in that building—somewhere downstairs! Swiftly he bolted from the laboratory and sped along the corridor to the rear of the building, where a stairway led to the basement. Room after room he searched frantically—but there was nobody on that basement floor.

Downstairs.... That must mean farther down—in the sub-cellar.

Instantly he was on his way, catfooting down to the lower level—to stop like one transfixed when he heard the sound of voices. One of those voices he would recognize anywhere in the world. Diane's!

"Don't listen to them!" she was begging. "Let them do what they please to me! I won't have you betray your trust!"

"But what does it matter, Diane?" That was Andrew Warren's voice, broken and discouraged. "The New Dawn can't be stopped. Washington is in their hands. What use to throw away your young life?"

Those voices were coming from just ahead, around the next bend in the corridor. Jimmy could picture the devilment that was being staged there. Gun in hand, he silently sped forward, turned into that corridor—and then it was as if the sub-cellar fairly rained men upon him. From every side they seemed to come, yellow-uniformed New Dawn storm troopers who launched themselves upon him and overwhelmed him by sheer numbers.

Dazed and panting, Jimmy was lifted to his feet and dragged down that corridor—into a low-vaulted room where the Devil himself seemed to be at play!

THE CENTER of that room seemed in imminent danger of collapsing. The ceiling, cracked and split wide by the explosion that had nearly ended Jimmy's life that night in Norman King's laboratory, was held up by a rickety looking scaffolding which had for its keystone a metal post in the center of the floor. Tied to that post was Diane Elliot, a mound of sticks and kindling piled around her feet!

Sitting helpless in a chair facing her was President Andrew Warren. Over him stood Calvin Hubbard, the man who had been his trusted confidant and adviser. Hubbard, his face twisted into lines of wolfish triumph, now lorded it there, surrounded by more than a score of his New Dawn storm troopers! He was desperately trying to bluff his way into the victory his routed army had not accomplished—to snatch victory out of defeat by this traitorous seizure of the Chief Executive!

"That's a lie, sir!" Jimmy shouted the moment they thrust him into the underground room. "The New Dawn is not victorious. We routed them. Morgan's men are wiping out the stragglers now. There is nothing left of the New Dawn—nothing but this handful of traitors who have been at work behind your back!"

Andrew Warren's eyes widened and he flashed a look at his Secretary of War. That glance was all that was necessary. Calvin Hubbard's rage-twisted face was its own confession.

"So you managed to rout a few thousand stupid storm troopers," Hubbard sneered, "and now think that will end the New Dawn. You fool, we are the New Dawn—not that rabble you put to flight. And this is where the New Dawn takes over the

182

American government and consolidates it with the New Dawn empire of the world!"

As that voice throbbed with mad gloating it rang reminiscently in Jimmy's ears. Then he placed it—on that night-club boat anchored on the Pittsburgh shore of the Monongahela! This was the unseen man whose voice he had heard gloating over a wild dream of world empire!

He was not the American double of Evan Carliotti. But that strapping fellow with the broad face who stood behind him— *that* face would readily take the mustache and goatee, gray wig and leonine aspect of the European Machiavelli....

"I knew that they were lying, Jimmy!" Diane cried with a thrill of happiness that took no cognizance of her own peril. "They have been trying to make the President sign a complete surrender and resign his office—"

"And that is exactly what Andy Warren is going to do," Calvin Hubbard cut in bruskly. "He is going to sign these documents now or we will have to try the persuasion we promised—only now we will make the program more comprehensive. Tie Warren and Operator 5 up there beside the girl," he ordered his troopers. "Stack more wood around them, and then we'll see whether he will sign or roast to death. Unless, of course, one of them should accidentally tug that pole lose and bring the sagging ceiling down on their heads!"

Jimmy tried to struggle, but he had no chance against such numbers. Andrew Warren had not the strength to offer much assistance. Quickly they were dragged to the metal post and tied up beside Diane—while Jimmy trembled for fear their tugging might tear the flimsy prop loose at any moment and bring death roaring down on her head.

He was helpless there against the pillar, helpless even to move without endangering the lives of all three of them. But there might still be a chance—even now when one of those leering devils lit a kindling taper and thrust it into the heaped-up fagots. Instantly, the dry wood caught fire. Smoke wreathed up and flames crackled.

"How about the signatures, Andy?" Calvin Hubbard taunted, while Jimmy Christopher desperately considered bringing the roof down on their heads in the hope of snaring that traitorous devil in his own trap. "It really is lots wiser to sign while you can—for in a little while we won't need your signature. You will be dead and I will seize the Presidency anyway. Better to be able to come to my inauguration—"

But suddenly Calvin Hubbard's face froze in a mask of surprise, then utter terror. The words died on his lips—and before he could move a black hole suddenly appeared in the center of his forehead... a hole that spouted blood as he pitched forward on the floor of that explosion-dinning chamber!

Calvin Hubbard was dead, and in a moment every one of those traitorous underlings who surrounded him knew that they were doomed. Wide-eyed, terrified, they gaped at the doorway which suddenly was filled with men. Tim Donovan stood there, a smoking automatic in his hand, a crowd of government clerks pressed in behind him. They blasted death into that precarious vault.

"Cut them down!" Tim's voice shouted above the thunder.

"These are no misguided working men—these are the lowest traitors who ever tried to tear down America!"

SOME OF those storm troopers tried to resist, but they were not equipped with their bullet-proof masks—and Tim's men shot at their faces. Mercilessly he drove them across the sub-cellar, his face grim, his eyes as cold as those of an executioner who takes the life of a convicted murderer. They died there, every one of those renegades who had hidden in public office while they plotted to overthrow their government—Calvin Hubbard and Henry Pfeiffer and all their breed....

Before that execution was finished Tim was at Jimmy Christopher's side, tramping out the mounting blaze and untying the prisoners.

"Once more, all I can say is thank God for Tim Donovan and those pals of yours," Jimmy said as he clasped Tim's hand. "But how—"

"How did we manage to get here?" Tim grinned. "That's because I have been keeping a headquarters of my own. One of us has been on the job there constantly, ready to answer the phone. Doc King knew that, so he managed to get in a call to us before he passed out. I got the rest together—and here we are."

That was all, but as Jimmy looked over that corpse-littered room he realized that it was Tim Donovan who had written the end to the New Dawn. Calvin Hubbard, he realized now, had been the figurehead, the traitor who was working from within—a cat's-paw in the hands of wily Evan Carliotti.

"And that husky, square-faced fellow—" Jimmy bent over him, turned up the dead face of Henry Pfeiffer, held it that way while he took a white mustache and goatee from the man's pocket and held them in place, studying the still features—"he was the American double who had been carrying out the master-plotter's orders!"

**THAT WAS** the end of the New Dawn in America. Once the myth of the deathless men was exploded, General Morgan's troops had no trouble routing the untrained and leaderless mobs, who disintegrated entirely after they had turned on Wladek Riegel and cold-bloodedly murdered him.

The end of the New Dawn in America—but it was not the end of Evan Carliotti. And while he lived the liberties which men cherish and give their lives for would be safe nowhere in the world. Carliotti was checked for the present, but Operator 5 wondered how long he would remain quiescent; how long he would leave America in peace....

Those grim thoughts were in his mind the day President Warren summoned him to the White House to witness a simple ceremony that was Operator 5's testimonial of gratitude. The other five who had a part in that ceremony were Tim Donovan and the four survivors of the five youths who had followed him to Europe. As they stood there, square-shouldered and sober-faced and held up their left hands, President Warren slipped onto the third finger of each a curiously shaped ring bearing on its crest a death's-head and the numeral "5"—and containing in its hollow center enough mighty explosive to rend a building asunder.

"Because you have proved yourselves worthy, because we trust you implicitly, and because it is upon men like you that the

## THE DAWN THAT SHOOK THE WORLD

United States of America must depend in the years to come," Andrew Warren concluded his presentation, "I present you with these rings—copies of the ring of your chief. May you wear them as honorably as he!"

AUTHOR'S NOTE: Evan Carliotti's menacing shadow seemed to cast its incredible length over the entire world, but it was in America that it threatened to obliterate every ray of hope and light. For the peace that settled over this country was not of long duration, and it was soon wiped out in an extraordinary and fearsome type of invasion. America had held out her arms in welcome to the persecuted citizens of the Old World who now fled to the land of liberty. But, once they reached our shores, instead of gratitude they returned evil for good—bringing the United States to the very brink of disaster, and compelling Operator 5 and his aides to wage the strangest battle ever fought on freedom's shores. The next installment will chronicle that amazing episode in American history.

## ACE G-MAN

- ❏ #1: The Suicide Squad Reports for Death $14.95
- ❏ #2: Coffins for the Suicide Squad $14.95
- ❏ #3: Shells for the Suicide Squad $14.95
- ❏ #4: The Suicide Squad in Corpse-Town $14.95
- ❏ #5: Wanted–In Three Pine Coffins $14.95
- ❏ #6: The Suicide Squad's Dawn Patrol $14.95
- ❏ #7: Targets for the Flaming Arrow $16.95

## OPERATOR 5

- ❏ #1: The Masked Invasion $13.95
- ❏ #2: The Invisible Empire $13.95
- ❏ #3: The Yellow Scourge $13.95
- ❏ #4: The Melting Death $13.95
- ❏ #5: Cavern of the Damned $13.95
- ❏ #6: Master of Broken Men $13.95
- ❏ #7: Invasion of the Dark Legions $13.95
- ❏ #8: The Green Death Mists $13.95
- ❏ #9: Legions of Starvation $13.95
- ❏ #10: The Red Invader $13.95
- ❏ #11: The League of War-Monsters $13.95
- ❏ #12: The Army of the Dead $13.95
- ❏ #13: March of the Flame Marauders $13.95
- ❏ #14: Blood Reign of the Dictator $13.95
- ❏ #15: Invasion of the Yellow Warlords $13.95
- ❏ #16: Legions of the Death Master $13.95
- ❏ #17: Hosts of the Flaming Death $13.95
- ❏ #18: Invasion of the Crimson Death Cult $13.95
- ❏ #19: Attack of the Blizzard Men $13.95
- ❏ #20: Scourge of the Invisible Death $13.95
- ❏ #21: Raiders of the Red Death $13.95
- ❏ #22: War-Dogs of the Green Destroyer $13.95
- ❏ #23: Rockets From Hell $13.95
- ❏ #24: War-Masters from the Orient $13.95
- ❏ #25: Crime's Reign of Terror $13.95
- ❏ #26: Death's Ragged Army $13.95
- ❏ #27: Patriots' Death Battalion $13.95
- ❏ #28: The Bloody Forty-five Days $13.95
- ❏ #29: America's Plague Battalions $13.95
- ❏ #30: Liberty's Suicide Legions $13.95
- ❏ #31: Siege of the Thousand Patriots $13.95
- ❏ #32: Patriots' Death March $14.95
- ❏ #33: Revolt of the Lost Legions $14.95
- ❏ #34: Drums of Destruction $14.95
- ❏ #35: The Army Without a Country $14.95
- ❏ #36: The Bloody Frontiers $14.95
- ❏ #37: The Coming of the Mongol Hordes $14.95
- ❏ #38: The Siege That Brought Black Death $16.95
- ❏ #39: Revolt of the Devil Men $16.95
- ❏ #40: The Suicide Battalion $16.95
- ❏ #41: The Day of the Damned $16.95
- ❏ **NEW:** #42: The Dawn That Shook the World $16.95

## RED FINGER

- ❏ #1: Second-Hand Death $24.95

## G-8 AND HIS BATTLE ACES

- ❏ #1: The Bat Staffel $13.95

## CAPTAIN COMBAT

- ❏ #1: The Sky Beast of Berlin $13.95
- ❏ #2: Red Wings For the Blood Battalion $13.95
- ❏ #3: Low Ceiling For Nazi Hell Hawks $13.95

## DUSTY AYRES AND HIS BATTLE BIRDS

- ❏ #1: Black Lightning! $13.95
- ❏ #2: Crimson Doom $13.95
- ❏ #3: The Purple Tornado $13.95
- ❏ #4: The Screaming Eye $13.95
- ❏ #5: The Green Thunderbolt $13.95
- ❏ #6: The Red Destroyer $13.95
- ❏ #7: The White Death $13.95
- ❏ #8: The Black Avenger $13.95
- ❏ #9: The Silver Typhoon $13.95
- ❏ #10: The Troposphere F-S $13.95
- ❏ #11: The Blue Cyclone $13.95
- ❏ #12: The Tesla Raiders $13.95

## MAVERICKS

- ❏ #1: Five Against the Law $12.95
- ❏ #2: Mesquite Manhunters $12.95
- ❏ #3: Bait for the Lobo Pack $12.95
- ❏ #4: Doc Grimson's Outlaw Posse $12.95
- ❏ #5: Charlie Parr's Gunsmoke Cure $12.95

## THE MYSTERIOUS WU FANG

- ❏ #1: The Case of the Six Coffins $12.95
- ❏ #2: The Case of the Scarlet Feather $12.95
- ❏ #3: The Case of the Yellow Mask $12.95
- ❏ #4: The Case of the Suicide Tomb $12.95
- ❏ #5: The Case of the Green Death $12.95
- ❏ #6: The Case of the Black Lotus $12.95
- ❏ #7: The Case of the Hidden Scourge $12.95

## THE SECRET 6

- ❏ #1: The Red Shadow $13.95
- ❏ #2: House of Walking Corpses $13.95
- ❏ #3: The Monster Murders $13.95
- ❏ #4: The Golden Alligator $13.95

## CAPTAIN ZERO

- ❏ #1: City of Deadly Sleep $13.95
- ❏ #2: The Mark of Zero! $13.95
- ❏ #3: The Golden Murder Syndicate $13.95